A THEATER TO DIE FOR

A WONDERLAND BOOKS COZY MYSTERY

BOOK TWO

M.P. BLACK

For all my bookish friends

CHAPTER 1

"*D*id you see this?" Ona Rodriguez slapped a folded newspaper down on the bookstore counter. She unfolded the paper and read the headline of an article aloud, "Death Trap Bookstore Transforms into Wonderland."

"Is it—?"

Alice Hartford reached out and snatched the paper from Ona, making her friend laugh. Ona wore an eye-patch with red rhinestones that glittered in the light from the bookstore lamps. It somehow made her look even more excited.

Alice scanned the article. It was down at the bottom of the page, tucked into the corner, and only two paragraphs long. But it didn't matter. A major city newspaper had written a favorable review of her little bookstore.

She read the review and then read it again. It mentioned her as, "The runaway bride who endeared herself to the community by solving a local murder case." More importantly, the journalist called the bookstore, "An oasis for book lovers, and despite its tiny setting—or because of it—well worth a visit to this off-the-beaten-track town."

"Imagine if we can get more reviews like this," Alice said. "Imagine what it will do for Blithedale."

Ona grinned, apparently as excited about it as Alice.

"Just wait till we open for the Blithedale Future Fund applications," Ona said.

Alice said nothing. She looked away, hoping she wouldn't blush. The three friends—Alice, Ona, and Becca—were meeting this Sunday afternoon to discuss the Blithedale Future Fund and the upcoming applications for new loans.

Alice had been keeping a big secret from Ona and Becca, and in the days ahead of their meeting, she'd been so sure they would approve of the work she'd done. Now she was beginning to doubt herself.

"I know what you're thinking," Ona said.

Alice's gut tightened. "You do?"

"Sure. You're thinking the process I designed for applications is overly formal—that it's bureaucratic. But it'll make it'll easier in the long run."

"Was it hard when you chose to support my bookstore?"

"Oh, no. It was easy." Ona smiled. "Easiest decision I ever made. But this is different. We're opening up to anyone with an idea. We'll be flooded with applicants. And we want it to be open and inclusive, don't you agree?"

Alice nodded, her lips pressed together.

Ona said, "Once we've helped more local businesses, the newspapers will be buzzing. And, for once, the stories won't be about murder. They'll be about the Blithedale Future Fund. Speaking of the fund, where's Becca?"

Ona dug into a pocket and brought out an old-fashioned pocket watch, opening it and checking the time.

"It's past 5 pm. She'd better hurry."

She shut the watch with a snap and slipped it into her pocket again.

"We've got a lot to talk about if we're going to open for applications next week."

Trying to hide her emotions, Alice dug into her box of book donations, which she'd been sorting when Ona walked in.

Alice had held off telling them about Dorothy Bowers and the Blithedale Theater—and how she'd encouraged Dorothy to apply.

All right, she admitted to herself, *I did more than encourage her.*

Without telling Becca and Ona, she'd contacted Dorothy, owner of the Blithedale Theater, and suggested that Blithedale would benefit if the movie theater thrived. The theater was old-fashioned and poorly attended. Everyone said so. The town needed a cultural hotspot. She was sure Becca and Ona would agree.

But she hadn't asked them before contacting Dorothy. She hadn't mentioned it after she and Dorothy met for coffee at Bonsai & Pie to discuss the matter. Nor after Dorothy called her to accept Alice's invitation to present a revitalization plan to the Future Fund, with the assumption that Alice, Becca, and Ona would support the idea.

The thought of keeping secrets from her new friends made her stomach churn, but, she told herself, she had a good reason to go it alone.

Wonderland Books.

Set in a 400-square foot, log-cabin tiny house on Blithedale's Main Street, Wonderland Books stood on the ground where Alice's mom had once run a bookstore. Before she got cancer and sold the store. Before she died. Before Alice moved in with her aunt and uncle—far from Blithedale.

From the age of 9, she'd felt disconnected from who she really was.

Leaving her fiancé at the altar and fleeing to Blithedale

changed all that, and even though the old bookstore was gone, the Blithedale Future Fund gave her the support to revive it as Wonderland Books.

Let's be honest, she told herself, *Becca and Ona gave me the financial support I needed.*

Her friends had given her a loan on terms that no bank would ever give, drawing on their own funds and additional support from community members to establish the Blithedale Future Fund for the purpose. Ona had built and donated the tiny house. And Alice?

I've done nothing...

Alice grew up self-reliant. She couldn't accept charity forever, even if the fund's support did come in the form of a loan. Becca and Ona meant well. But their help, their generosity—it reminded her of how her fiancé, Rich, had almost suffocated her with his attention.

The memory made her shudder.

No, it's time to stop taking so much—it's time for me to give back.

She only hoped her friends would understand when she revealed her plans tonight.

Besides, it's not like I'm doing this without any guidance.

Next to the box of donated books lay an old, leatherbound notebook. She touched its well-worn cover. It had belonged to Old Mayor Townsend whose statue stood outside the Pemberley Inn, Ona's Jane Austen-inspired boutique hotel, and it contained the old mayor's vision for the town.

Ona gestured toward the book. "Still reading the old mayor's ideas for Blithedale?"

"His ideas are so—so—what's the word…?"

"Outdated?"

"Prescient."

"Fancy word for a lucky guess."

Old Mayor Townsend's vision was anything but a lucky guess. Sure, some ideas wouldn't work today—like his insistence that Main Street should be widened to accommodate a tram—but his basic vision made even more sense in the 21st century: He'd wanted to create a thriving community that offered everything a person might need within walking distance, not least of which was the nature: Blithedale lay nestled in the woods, with the beautiful Hiawatha River splashing lazily through town.

"Blithedale has great potential," Alice said. "Old Mayor Townsend saw that. If we can help fix up some of the rundown buildings and support the struggling businesses…"

"Then we can get a hundred more reviews like this," Ona said.

"Reviews like what?" Becca swept into the bookstore with a Tupperware in her arms and tote bag over her shoulder. "Don't tell me you got a negative customer review."

"Check this out," Ona said as Becca put her Tupperware down on a bench.

Becca Frye owned the What the Dickens Diner, Blithedale's main watering hole, where everyone gathered for meals and gossip. She shook the tote bag off her broad shoulder and a gap-toothed grin spread across her face.

"A review like this would never have appeared in *The Blithedale Record*."

Ona shook her head. "Not in a million years."

The Blithedale Record, the local newspaper, had shut down. After being involved in a scandal that sent his brother to prison, the newspaper's owner and sole journalist, Todd Townsend, had skipped town.

"I do sometimes wonder what happened to him," Alice said.

Ona raised her one visible eyebrow, the other being hidden by her eyepatch. "I hope you're not losing sleep over

Todd Townsend. I'm sure he's halfway across the country, running a new tabloid and spinning lies."

"Or he's learned from his mistakes and he's turned over a new leaf."

"You're an optimist and an angel, Alice," Becca said, smiling at her. "Like your mom was. And maybe you're right. You know what Estella says in *Great Expectations*?"

Alice and Ona exchanged a smile, and they both shook their heads. Becca was always quoting Charles Dickens, her favorite author, and the central theme of her diner.

"She says, 'I have been bent and broken, but—I hope—into a better shape.'"

"You have a Dickens quote for every occasion," Ona said with a laugh.

"And donuts for every occasion, too."

Becca bent over the Tupperware and pulled off its lid. Alice and Ona made ooh sounds. Inside were rows of donuts —powdered, glazed, and jelly-filled. And digging into the tote, Becca produced a thermos and three cups.

"Decaf coffee. You can't talk business without coffee."

She set the three cups on a bookshelf.

Alice eyed them, butterflies fluttering in her stomach. She checked the time on her phone. It was 5:15 pm. She should tell them everything before Dorothy arrived at half past.

"We're going to need a fourth cup," she said.

Becca and Ona looked at her.

"A fourth cup?" Becca said.

"Who else is coming?" Ona said.

Alice took a deep breath. "You know how much the Blithedale Future Fund's support has meant to me. Ona, you gifted me one of your beautiful tiny houses. And with the support of locals, I've been able to stock my bookshop. But if it hadn't been for the fund's financial aid, I would never have been able to afford the property. Without your support, none of this—" She gestured around at the rafters, the book-shelves. "—would exist."

"It's a loan," Ona said with a shrug. "No biggie."

"But it is a big deal. A huge deal. And while I pay back my loan, I also need to pay back in other ways."

"Sweetie," Becca said. "You don't need to pay back anything."

"But I do," Alice insisted. "And I'm starting by helping an important business in Blithedale take a leap forward."

Ona nodded. "Great. That's why we're here, isn't it? To figure out the applications for the next round of support? So we can review applicants and select the next recipient."

"See, the things is…" Alice bit her lip. "I've already identi-fied the next recipient."

"You've done what?"

Becca put a hand on Ona's arm. "Tell us more, Alice. We're listening."

Alice described how she'd studied Old Mayor Townsend's notes on Blithedale's development, and one point he kept coming back to was the idea of investing in the spaces where people congregate.

"He mentions the church. He mentions the eatery, which is where the diner stands today. And he mentions the theater." She tapped the cover of the notebook with a finger. "It's all in here. If we revitalize the theater, it will not only create a hub for entertainment in town, it will also attract people from outside. So that's why I contacted Dorothy Bowers…"

Ona frowned. "You contacted Dorothy?"

"Well, we hadn't announced that the fund was accepting applications, so I got ahead of the game. I called her. I asked her what she'd do if she had funding to revitalize the theater."

"What did she do, yell at you and hang up?"

"She can be a tough cookie," Becca said. "She rubs a lot of people the wrong way."

"She wasn't rude at all," Alice said. "In fact, she got excited. She said she knew exactly what to do, and that she'd present her full plans to us."

"We can always listen to what she has to say," Becca said. "It's not as if we've promised her anything."

"Well…" Alice felt her face grow hot. "I did meet with her for a coffee and kind of encouraged her…"

"I can't believe it," Ona said, arms across her chest, a deep frown on her face.

Alice checked her phone, afraid to look Ona in the eyes. "Dorothy will be here any minute now."

Ona lapsed into silence. Becca unscrewed the thermos top and poured coffee into three cups. She handed one to Ona, one to Alice, and then took one herself.

"Alice," she said. "You should've told us."

"I know, I know, but—"

"Not because Ona and I somehow decide what happens. In fact, we don't want to decide. No, it's because you can't handle the whole thing by yourself. No one can."

"Yeah," Ona said. "It's a lot."

Alice flinched inwardly. *They're my friends,* she reminded herself. But another voice in her weighed in: *So, why don't they think I'm competent enough to handle Dorothy's plans?*

"Let's see what Dorothy says," she mumbled.

Ona and Becca exchanged a look. Then Becca said, "Good idea. Let's see what she says, and then we can take it from there."

Ona sipped her coffee. Becca sat down on one of the small benches next to the bookshelves, and she grabbed a donut and nibbled at its edges. An unusual silence descended on them as they waited, and Alice busied herself with her box of donations.

After she'd opened Wonderland Books, many local citizens had emptied their attics and basements and garages of old paperbacks and hardbacks, eager to help her with stock. Most of the books were junk. Tattered copies of thrillers that no longer sold. Mildew-stained editions of abridged classics. A dozen *Merck Manuals* from 1992.

But occasionally she found treasure.

She laid one such book on the small counter. A first edition of A. A. Milne's *The House at Pooh Corner*. A tear in the dust jacket and a cracked spine were unforgivable sins in the world of pristine, auctionable first editions, but only a handful of pages had stains, and to a genuine lover of the Hundred Acre Wood, this copy would be a delight.

Alice flipped through the book. Usually she would've taken great pleasure in the classic illustrations. But she was too aware of the awkward silence in the bookstore.

Once Dorothy gets here and they see her plans, everything will be all right again.

Further down in the box, she found a badly beat-up first edition of the Nancy Drew book, *Mystery of Crocodile Island*. This one she'd keep for herself. She loved Nancy Drew. In fact, she adored all kinds of books—her childhood favorite was *Alice's Adventures in Wonderland*—but once she'd discovered mysteries as a kid, she'd been smitten. Her mom had solved several mysteries in Blithedale, endearing herself even more to the locals. According to Becca, Alice had the same knack—or compulsion—for putting her nose in police matters.

The last discovery was a beautiful box set of L. Frank Baum's Oz books—all 14 in the series, starting with *The Wonderful Wizard of Oz* and ending with *Glinda of Oz*. It wasn't a first edition, but it would make someone happy— whether that was a collector or a kid.

She sorted through the rest of the books. Some good, mostly bad. And then checked the time again.

"Is Dorothy the punctual type?" she asked.

"Dorothy is—" Ona paused. "—the interesting type."

Her tone of voice suggested that "interesting" was a euphemism.

"Are you telling me she's flakey?"

"Oh, no," Becca said. "Quite the opposite. If Dorothy decides to do something, she's like a bull seeing red. Nothing will stop her."

Alice looked at her watch. "Well, something clearly has. She's late."

Ona shrugged. "Dorothy runs on Dorothy time."

They drank coffee, ate donuts, and waited for their guest of honor, and with every minute that passed, Alice felt more and more uncomfortable. She couldn't help but remember what her friends had said about her not being capable of handling this kind of thing. She needed to prove she could give back to them.

"I'll give Dorothy a call," she said.

But the phone rang and rang, and Dorothy didn't answer.

Finally, Alice put her phone away. She was so ashamed of how this was turning out that she wasn't able to look her friends in the eyes. She hurried out from behind the counter.

"I'll be right back," she said. "I'm going to find Dorothy—you stay here."

CHAPTER 2

The Blithedale Theater's marquee advertised three movies on Saturday: a matinee with an animated film for kids and a *Wizard of Oz* singalong. But next to that was the word, "canceled." Below it, the big black letters said,

NEW: *GREASE* SINGALONG.

But that had been last night. Today, Sunday, the theater was closed.

Alice knocked on the glass doors to the theater. She shielded her eyes with a hand and peered into the lobby. Carpeted floors. A concession stand. But no movement.

She hadn't been inside since moving back to Blithedale, but she had vague memories of going to the movies with her mom.

She tugged at the doors, trying each one. Then trying them again.

"They're locked."

Alice turned. Ona was leaning against one of the walls

where glass cases displayed posters of the latest movies—all classics. *Grease* seemed to be the closest to a modern movie.

"I'm sure Dorothy will be right with us," Alice said.

"Becca got called back to the diner," Ona said. "A whole convoy of truckers arrived, plus the fly-fishing club has its monthly meetup, so Susan needed a hand. So I figured I'd follow you to see if *you* needed a hand."

"I'm fine," Alice said. "Really."

She tugged at the doors once more, and knocked again.

Ona sighed. "Why don't we try the back?"

An alleyway ran alongside the building. As they headed down the passageway, Ona said, "Bummer that Dorothy canceled the *Wizard of Oz* singalong."

"Looks like she put on *Grease* instead, and honestly, who can resist a little 'Greased Lightnin'?"

"The Oz fans?"

"True—Olivia Newton-John isn't the same as Judy Garland, especially after the makeover at the end of the movie."

"Wait," Ona said, "Judy Garland gets a makeover at the end of *Wizard of Oz*?"

It felt good to joke again. The awkward silence between them had vanished, and they were back to being friends. Alice was aware that Ona was giving her a second chance.

There's that generosity again, she thought.

They emerged from the alley into a parking lot. Trash cans stood lined up against the brick wall of the theater. A metal staircase led to a back door.

After climbing the stairs, Ona pulled the handle, and the door swung open.

"If the door's open, Dorothy must still be at work," she said.

"I thought there weren't any movies on Sundays."

"There aren't. But Dorothy's like Becca—she works seven

days a week. The theater's her baby. It's been in the family for generations. The theater goes back to the vaudeville age."

The back door opened onto a stairwell. A sign with an arrow pointing upward said, "Projectionist Booth."

To the right, a sign on a door said, "Office." Alice knocked on that one. No answer.

She opened the door and peered into a small office. A desk with a computer. A bookshelf with ring binders. Everything was tidy.

There was no sign of Dorothy, though.

On a cork board, pieces of card featured tasks written with a thick marker pen. One card said, "Present plan to Future Fund."

Alice frowned. If Dorothy was so task-oriented, and she'd put the Future Fund on her board, why'd she fail to show up?

"Let's look in the lobby," Ona said.

Another door in the stairwell, also clearly marked, led them to the lobby Alice had seen through the front doors. The carpeted space smelled of popcorn and burned sugar. She breathed it in and with it, a wellspring of happy childhood memories bubbled up.

"I remember coming here as a kid," she said, "with my mom."

She ran a hand along the brass-edging on the long concession counter. The popcorn machine was empty of popcorn. Above head, a sign from a bygone era listed the refreshments: "Hot dogs, popcorn, peanuts, candy, soft drinks."

At the end of the concession stand stood an old, wood-paneled phone booth. And next to that stood an old gumball machine.

A memory came back to her: Her mom pressing a coin into her hand.

"Here you go, sweetie. Go get some candy."

Occasionally, these memories of the past would grow clearer, as if she were reclaiming them after half a lifetime of burying them. She remembered going to the movies and watching *The Land Before Time*. It only occurred to her years later that the animated film was already old by the time she watched it.

Who cared? She had such fond memories of sitting next to her mom, sharing popcorn, holding hands.

"You feel her, don't you?" Ona said, softly.

Alice nodded, at a loss for words.

"She's with you now."

Alice knew it to be true. Ever since she'd come back to Blithedale, and especially since she'd opened Wonderland Books, she'd felt her mom. Not like a spirit that talked to her. Not like a ghost. Though when these memories welled up, there was the sensation of being together. Of no longer feeling so alone.

Ona slipped an arm around her shoulders and pulled her close.

"Are you all right?"

"I've never been better," Alice said, and shrugged out of her friend's embrace. "But enough thinking about the past—let's go find Dorothy."

Ona suggested they check the upstairs booth, and they returned to the stairwell.

As they climbed the stairs, Ona said, "The theater's so quiet. Like no one's here. Maybe she or Mr. Gorny, the care-taker and projectionist, simply forgot to lock the back door."

"Mr. Gorny," Alice said, trying to remember. "A grumpy old guy?"

"That's right. Who knows how old the dude is. But he's been an old grumpy guy for a hundred years."

"I think I was a little afraid of him as a kid."

"You're not alone—Becca told me every kid in town grew

up being afraid of him. He's not just the caretaker and projectionist, he's also the usher, the concessionist, and the enforcer of movie theater etiquette. He barks at the kids if they run, a big no-no according to his rules."

They stepped into the projectionist booth, but it was empty, too. Or at least empty of people. A large projector with actual rolls of 35mm film pointed through a small window to the auditorium.

"Wow," Alice said. "Old school."

"The Bowers were traditionalists and resisted the changeover to digital." Ona gave the old projector a pat. "Incredibly, the theater kept right on using old film."

"I'm surprised it's even possible to find movies on 35mm film anymore."

"It's not easy. And it's not lucrative. Dorothy mostly shows old movies. Which everyone agrees is charming, and it's so wonderful that we have this old relic and blah blah blah. But when they want to watch a movie, they all drive to the nearest multiplex, because really, what they want to see is the latest Hollywood blockbuster."

Alice looked through the hole for the projector. The auditorium was dark. But even in the gloom, she could make out the rows of plush seats and the old stage. Framed by heavy drapery, it did look like a relic from a bygone era.

In the dim light, something on stage sparkled.

"What is that down there?"

Ona joined her at the tiny window, peering down at the dark stage.

"No idea. Let's turn on some lights."

Next to the projector, a table held an old-fashioned lighting console. A label on each slider identified its function. Alice stared at the sliders for a moment, chewing her lower lip, then found the right controls. She reached for a slider and pushed it up. Then another.

Through the little window, the auditorium lit up. Ona stepped over to the projector and looked down at the stage.

She gasped.

"What?" Alice asked.

"Look."

Alice joined her at the little window.

The auditorium glowed red. With the plush, red seats and heavy, crimson curtains draping the sides of the stage, it looked unreal. Like a strange dream. But Alice's eyes soon fastened on the sparkling objects on stage. A pair of shiny shoes.

A woman lay in the middle of the stage on her back, a metal pole with several heavy stage lights across her chest. A pool of dark, almost black blood spread around her head.

Alice stared at Ona and Ona stared back, wide-eyed.

She whispered, "Dorothy."

CHAPTER 3

"*N*ow, look here, it was obviously an accident," Chief of Police James Sapling, Jr. said. Everyone knew him as Chief Jimbo. And everyone also knew him as a man who would go to the moon and back to avoid arduous work. A murder investigation being the most arduous. "See that metal pole thingy? A rope held it in place, and that came loose, and the whole thing fell on her."

Alice, who sat in the front row of the auditorium, couldn't believe it. She couldn't believe that another murder had happened in Blithedale, that she'd found the body, and that, once again, Chief Jimbo was going to bungle the investigation, simply because he was too lazy—or timid—to take charge.

Next to her, Ona was shaking her head, clearly as disgusted with the situation as she was.

"A batten," the county coroner said from where he was crouched down by Dorothy's body.

"A what-now?"

"It's called a batten, Chief Jimbo. Among theater people. And I agree—it most definitely killed her."

17

Chief Jimbo beamed. "Then we're all good—right, Lenny?"

The county coroner, a man named Leonard—or Lenny—Stout, let out a long, weary sigh. He wore a gray suit that was so rumpled, he must've slept in it. His face was equally gray and rumpled. The only colorful things about him were his tie and socks, both of which featured a garish pattern of Winnie-the-Poohs.

He stood to his full height, his knees cracking, and he put a hand to his lower back. He said, "We're not all good, Chief Jimbo. We've got a dead woman and at least two unanswered questions."

Chief Jimbo frowned, looking worried. But at least he got out his pen and notepad, ready to jot down whatever Lenny was about to say.

"Number one," Lenny said, "how did that rope come loose, and why did it do so at the very moment Dorothy Bowers stood underneath that particular batten?"

Chief Jimbo scribbled notes.

"Number two: Why is the deceased wearing those?"

He pointed at the shoes. They were sneakers covered in bright red sequins that caught the light and shimmered.

Chief Jimbo looked up from his notes. "Uh, maybe because she liked sparkly shoes?"

"I knew Dorothy Bowers. So did you. Did you ever see her wear anything sparkly?"

While Chief Jimbo thought about that, Lenny provided the answer: "The woman didn't wear makeup or jewelry. Her favorite color was beige. She wouldn't be caught dead wearing shoes like that."

"Well, you say that, but—"

Lenny held up a hand. "Please, no jokes." Then he eyed Chief Jimbo critically. "Jimbo, maybe this is an appropriate time to call in help from the state police. I know it's hard to be responsible in a single-cop town. It was tough on your dad, too."

"But he never asked for help," Chief Jimbo said with pride. "Not once."

"I'm aware of that. Your father had many outstanding qualities as a cop. His lone wolf attitude was not one of them."

"I've got this, Lenny. Besides, I have all the support I need."

Chief Jimbo stuffed his pen and notepad into a pocket and pulled out, from another, a heavily dog-eared paperback.

Alice sighed. She knew the book well—Chief Jimbo was always referring to it: *The Police Chief Companion: 21 Days to Killing It On the Job*. Chief Jimbo had been reading and referencing the book for much longer than 21 days.

Before Chief Jimbo could quote his indispensable manual, a voice at the back of the auditorium turned everyone's heads.

"My God," a man cried out. "What happened?"

The man must've been in his eighties. His advanced age and a pair of bow legs didn't slow him as he hurried down the aisle toward the stage. Although none of her childhood fears surfaced, Alice could guess who he was—this was Mr. Gorny, the theater caretaker.

He struggled up the steps to the stage, and Lenny held out his hands to keep him back.

"You can't come up here, Mr. Gorny."

The old man looked at Dorothy and let out a volley of curses so colorful, Alice might've guessed he was a sailor.

"My dear Dorothy," he whispered. He sucked in a ragged breath. Then his brows furrowed, and he glared at the rigging, as if he were about to scold it. "That batten was well secured. Who did this?"

"Calm down," Chief Jimbo said. "No one did anything. This is a tragic accident."

"Tragic accident, my foot," Mr. Gorny snapped. He turned to Lenny. "How does it look to you?"

"Could be worse. Not sure how, but it could be."

"But you're not fool enough to think it was an accident, are you?"

Lenny gave a brief shake of his head.

"Good." Mr. Gorny rounded on Chief Jimbo. "You're an amateur, Jimbo, and I won't have you ruin this investigation. Someone obviously killed Dorothy. Murdered her. And I demand a proper investigation."

Chief Jimbo lowered his eyes, looking cowed. He fiddled with his paperback manual and muttered, "Yes, sir."

Alice leaned close to Ona to whisper.

"So, Mr. Gorny's responsible for the rigging?"

Ona nodded.

Apparently, Lenny had the same thought, because he said, "Mr. Gorny, you must've secured that rope. Could it have slipped?"

"No. Absolutely not. We run a tight ship."

"Could someone have tampered with it?"

"Maybe." Mr. Gorny gave it some thought, then shook his head. "But why would anyone want to do that? Who would want to hurt Dorothy? The Bowers have run this theater for generations—through two world wars and countless recessions. They've been a pillar of this society, bringing joy and laughter and—"

He seemed to choke up. His legs wobbled, and Alice feared he might fall.

Steadying himself with a deep breath, he gazed down at Dorothy, a wistful look on his face. But the wistful look soon darkened. "Who put those ridiculous shoes on her feet?"

"I wondered that, too," Lenny said. "Any ideas?"

Mr. Gorny shook his head.

But Alice had a thought.

"The singalong," she said, and the three men on stage turned toward her.

Mr. Gorny glared at her, as grumpy as if he'd been an actor on stage interrupted by an audience member.

"Singalong?" he said. "What singalong?"

"*The Wizard of Oz* singalong."

"I'm out of my depth," Lenny said. "Please explain."

Alice said, "There was a singalong planned for Saturday— an event where people watch *The Wizard of Oz* and sing along to the songs. Except it was cancelled. But my point is that in the old movie, Judy Garland wears ruby-red slippers and—"

She stopped herself. She'd just made another connection.

"What a coincidence," she said, "that a real-life Dorothy should be killed and then put in ruby-red shoes, like Dorothy in *The Wizard of Oz*."

"Coincidence," Mr. Gorny snorted.

"I agree." Lenny nodded. "I don't believe in coincidences."

Neither did Alice. She'd read enough Nancy Drew to tell a coincidence from a clue. Whoever killed Dorothy Bowers was sending a message.

CHAPTER 4

*T*he next morning, Alice woke early.

Even before she opened her eyes, a question boomed through her mind: *What will happen to the theater?* If Old Mayor Townsend was right, the theater was essential to making the town thrive. What would happen now that Dorothy was dead?

Alice rolled out of the canopy bed, pushed open the windows, and breathed in the fresh air.

A tapestry of trees spread across the hills and up the sides of the verdant mountains, stretching as far as the eye could see. The forest reached down to town, nearly swallowing it. Only the river and Main Street interrupted the dense trees.

Hiawatha River, snaking under the bridge that divided Main Street, sparkled in the early morning sun.

Main Street was already alive with the slow drift of cars and pedestrians meandering toward work. Kids congregated to catch school buses to larger towns with schools. (*Maybe the Blithedale Future Fund could get involved,* she thought. *The town would eventually need its own school...*) Most shops wouldn't open for another couple of hours, but leaning out, Alice could see people milling in and out of the diner.

She spun around and bounded into the bathroom. After a quick shower, she strung her hair into a pragmatic ponytail, brushed her teeth, and threw on a pair of jeans and a t-shirt that said, "The Book Was Better." She had a closet full of book-themed t-shirts and wore them with pride.

Leaving her room, she greeted the mannequin with the flannel waistcoat.

"Morning, Colonel Brandon."

She was staying in the so-called Colonel Brandon suite. She'd checked into the Pemberley Inn when she first came to Blithedale, and since then, hadn't checked out. Ona insisted she could stay as long as she wanted—for free—or at least until she found herself another home.

Alice hadn't been able to find a rental anywhere, and with all her savings tied up in the bookstore, she couldn't afford to buy a home. So she continued to live rent free. She helped out at the front desk and in the kitchen, when she could. But still, it was another way in which she felt indebted to her friend.

She took the grand old Victorian stairs two at a time, hurrying past the gilt-framed portraits of Jane Austen characters—from Emma Woodhouse to Charles Bingley—and landing in the reception with a thump.

"You're chipper this morning," Ona said, looking up from behind the reception desk.

"It's a beautiful day."

"And—?"

"And I'm hungry."

"And—?"

"And I want to go to the diner."

"And—?"

Alice sighed, caving in to Ona's persistent questioning.

"All right. I want to know what will happen to the theater now that Dorothy's gone."

"Right," Ona said. "And how about why someone killed her and put her in ruby-red sneakers?"

Alice shook her head. "I'm leaving this investigation to the pros. I just want to make sure the theater is safe."

"Whatever you say, Nancy Drew."

Ona insisted on joining Alice. A moment later, the two of them were heading down the front porch steps of the Victorian mansion. They passed the statue of Old Mayor Townsend on the street, and Alice gave him a cheerful wave.

They crossed the bridge and the driver of a passing car honked his horn. It was Thor, the handsome owner of the Woodlander, a tiny house bar nestled in the forest. They waved to him as he passed.

By the time they got to the What the Dickens Diner, they'd greeted a dozen people and stopped at least three times to chat, including with Esther Lucas, who ran the Love Again consignment store, and with Andrea Connor, whose cafe, Bonsai & Pie, sold the town's best pies—and, of course, the best bonsai trees, too.

Inside the diner, Becca and Susan, the waitress, were busy serving breakfast. A group of truck drivers sat at the counter, drinking coffee and eating pancakes, and talking about the weather, the traffic, and which classic rock songs never went out of fashion. They were having a heated argument about "Eye of the Tiger."

But it was the man in the white suit sitting alone in a booth that caught Alice's eye.

She nudged Ona.

"Let's go talk to Mayor MacDonald."

"Alice. Ona." Mayor MacDonald smiled as they approached, his smile only faltering a little when he said

Ona's name. They didn't always see eye to eye. "You're out and about early."

"So are you," Alice said, slipping onto the leatherette seat across from him. Ona joined her.

"Oh, it's like Mark Twain says, we old folks rise early because we've done so many mean things all our lives that we can't sleep anyway."

"Don't be silly. What mean things have you done?"

"They're mine to stew over."

He winked, showing just how unburdened by mean things he really was. He no doubt slept well at night, too. His quip had more to do with his love of Twain than anything else. In fact, the mayor had the same white mustache and white unruly hair as the creator of Tom Sawyer and Huckleberry Finn did in his later years. He usually wore a white suit, too. The overall effect was to make him the top candidate for a Mark Twain lookalike award.

He took a sip of coffee and eyed Alice and Ona from beneath his bushy white eyebrows, a sparkle of amusement in his eyes.

"It's not my natural charm that brings you ladies to my table, is it? You're curious about poor Dorothy Bowers." He held up a hand, and before Alice or Ona could say anything, he continued: "Well, I'm sorry to say that you—with your talent for being in the right place at the right time—probably know more than I do."

Alice said, "After Chief Jimbo took our statements, the county coroner shooed us away. And anyway, that's not—"

"Good old Lenny Stout. His suits may need ironing, but his integrity is as smooth as any you'll see. It's certainly less rumpled than Jimbo's. In fact, our chief of police is still insisting Dorothy's death was an accident."

"He's what?" Alice shook her head. "I can't believe it."

In fact, she could believe it. When she'd first come to

Blithedale, she'd witnessed a killer flee from a murder scene. Chief Jimbo flat out refused to believe her, claiming there was no evidence of foul play. He was allergic to murder investigations. But this time, she really would leave him to his work. She had to focus on the fate of the theater—and Blithedale as a whole.

Ona, clearly interested in the murder investigation, leaned forward. "Did the coroner say when he thought Dorothy died?"

"Most likely sometime between Saturday evening and Sunday morning. There was a showing of the musical *Grease*, a singalong, and people saw Dorothy then."

"What about Mr. Gorny?"

"Mr. Gorny is furious," Mayor MacDonald said. "He's threatening to call the state cops and get the FBI involved and raise hell with his congressman, all at the same time."

"Was he the last to see Dorothy alive?"

"He left while there were still *Grease* fans hanging around the lobby. Mr. Gorny usually goes home right after the Saturday night performance—he has some kind of regular commitment. Besides, Dorothy always stayed late. That woman spent most of her time at the theater."

Becca stopped by their table, smiling as she filled cups of coffee for each of them. Then she hurried off again, too busy to stop and chat.

Mayor MacDonald took a sip of coffee. "What a shame."

"That Dorothy's gone?" Ona asked.

Mayor MacDonald furrowed his bushy brows. "Oh, no. I didn't mean—well, of course, it's a tragedy. I meant more that we have another murder in our wonderful town. And who knows whether it will ever be solved."

"Because of Chief Jimbo?"

"'When a man is known to have no settled convictions of

his own,'" the mayor said, apparently quoting Twain, "'he can't convict other people.'"

He sighed. "The problem is the press. Once they get hold of this, we're in trouble. With Vince's death, the details weren't as colorful. Plus, the case got solved quickly—thanks to you." He gave Alice a nod. Then he shook his head gravely and said, "But with the sensational details of ruby-red sneakers and a body left center stage…and if Mr. Gorny gets his way and involves the FBI and others. Oh, boy. Then you can be sure Blithedale will be overrun by the media. Despite what people say, there is such a thing as bad press."

Ona sat back, shaking her head, too. "That does sound bad."

Alice, who'd been sipping her coffee, set down her cup. She was picturing vans from all the major networks down Main Street. Journalists crowding the diner. Morbid out-of-towners peering through windows, greedily ogling the "scene of the crime." That was how they'd view Blithedale, wasn't it? She shuddered. It could be a disaster.

But what can I do about it? Nothing.

She shook the dread off. Mayor MacDonald had painted a bleak picture—but that was all it was, a picture. She couldn't act on imaginary disasters. She'd better focus on where she could make a difference.

"What about the theater?" she asked the mayor. "What will happen to it now that Dorothy's gone?"

"Beau Bowers. Dorothy's good-for-nothing brother. The black sheep of the Bowers clan—and the last in line. He inherits everything."

"But does he know anything about running a theater?"

"As far as I know, nothing. The guy never took an interest in the family business as a kid. He got into all kinds of trouble. And then the drinking began…" Mayor MacDonald shook his head. "If you ask me, the guy will run the place into the ground. Or sell it to the highest bidder."

Alice and Ona looked at each other. They remembered all too well what happened when someone sold to the highest bidder. Blithedale's own Darrell Townsend, a developer, had wanted to raze most of the old buildings and erect strip malls and put in parking lots. Given the chance, he would've torn down the Blithedale Theater in a heartbeat.

Darrell might be in prison, but if the theater went up for sale, another greedy developer would undoubtedly swoop in. Alice couldn't let that happen.

CHAPTER 5

Beau Bowers lived north of town in a cabin in the woods.

Since she didn't own a car, Alice hoofed it out of town and up a northbound trail. She trekked deeper and deeper into the forest. Old oaks creaked. A bird somewhere screeched. A branch snapped, and Alice peered into the woods, sure she'd see someone moving among the trees. Goosebumps prickled her arms, and she rubbed them. But she didn't see anyone.

Mayor MacDonald had talked about Beau's drinking being "out of control," and how he'd fled to the woods when the family had disinherited him. He implied the man might be dangerous.

She caught herself wishing Ona was with her.

But she'd left Ona behind. In fact, she'd lied to her. Knowing Ona would want to tag along, Alice had told her she needed to open the bookstore.

This whole Blithedale Theater project is a disaster, she told herself. *It's my own fault. I reached out to Dorothy. I encouraged her plans. Now, I have to find a way to fix this mess and show Becca and Ona that I can make this Future Fund stuff a success.*

So Alice had said goodbye to Ona at the diner. She'd gone back to the store and hung a sign on the door that said, "Be back soon."

Which made her feel doubly guilty—for lying to Ona and for neglecting her store. The store her friends had paid for.

Technically, they haven't paid for it, she reminded herself. *It's a loan from the Blithedale Future Fund.*

But no matter what the loan agreement said, she knew that the money was a kind of gift from her friends.

The path among the trees twisted, and she came upon a dirt road. It was deeply rutted, no doubt an old logging road. After a while, the road ran through a clearing in the woods, vanishing into the depths of the forest. In the middle of the clearing sat a log cabin, about the size of one of Ona's tiny houses.

Outside the cabin stood a man with an ax.

Alice came to a dead stop.

The morning light was in Alice's eyes. She squinted.

The man was skinny, yet the bulk of his body looked big and square. With the ax resting by his side, he reminded her of the Tin Woodman from *The Wonderful Wizard of Oz*, or the Tin Man, as he was called in the movie.

She blinked. And then moved to the side to get the sun out of her eyes and saw that the man was just a man. He wore a hunter's vest with pockets, which made his otherwise skinny body looked bulky.

She'd interrupted Beau Bowers in splitting wood. But if he'd been active a moment ago, he now stood still, as frozen as the rusted Tin Woodman that Dorothy and the Scarecrow found in *The Wonderful Wizard of Oz*.

He stared off into the distance. Then a flash of yellow took flight from a branch and vanished into the woods. It broke the spell. Beau turned away from the bird he'd been watching and stared straight at Alice.

"Yellow warbler." He narrowed his eyes. "I recognize you. You're the owner of that new bookstore—the one who solved the murder."

"I'm Alice."

"You're here about Dorothy, aren't you?"

She was taken aback by his directness. Yet there was nothing brusque about him. If anything, he was so soft spoken it seemed he treated the forest as one would a library.

He didn't wait for her to answer, but turned on his heels and trudged to the cabin. He set the ax down, resting it against the wall, stomped his boots to free them of mud, and then stepped inside.

Alice hesitated.

"Guess I follow," she muttered to herself.

Inside the cabin, it was gloomy. Only two small windows provided any light, and curtains kept the sunlight at bay. Age had darkened the hardwood beams. A small stone fireplace dominated one side, a single bed the opposite. In the middle of the small space sat a table with four chairs. At the back was a tiny kitchen, with a sink, a stove, and a small refrigerator. But no oven. And a rack held a few plates, bowls, cups, and cutlery, just enough for one person. There were stacks of books on the floor as well as a battered guitar in the corner.

The overall impression was of a modest and, above all, tidy home. And, Alice noted, free of any bottles of booze. Though maybe he hid them.

Beau stood by the kitchen counter. He put a kettle on the gas stove.

"Please sit. Coffee or tea?"

When Alice said coffee, he got out a jar with instant and spooned the grounds into two mugs. Meanwhile, Alice sat at the table, making sure to stay on the side closest to the front door.

A minute later, Beau handed her a coffee mug and sat down with his own.

Alice wasn't sure what she'd expected. A raging man flinging whiskey bottles at her? A giant hulk, half-sedated with drink? A drunken wreck who had no idea what was going on? Instead, Beau was a droopy-eyed man in his forties, with the kind of melancholy face you saw in paintings of Catholic saints.

He said, "Chief Jimbo called me and told me what happened."

Alice offered her condolences.

He lifted his shoulders in a shrug. "I'm sad she's gone, and it's awful that anyone would kill another human being. But Dorothy and I were never close."

Alice took a sip of the coffee. It was good and strong. She tried to think of a delicate way to approach the subject. "Dorothy inherited the family business…"

"And I didn't," he said. "Yes, my family disapproved of me. I gave them lots of things to disapprove of, including my drinking. They hurt me. I felt rejected and alone. But I don't blame them. And I certainly never blamed Dorothy."

Alice didn't need to know about Beau's relationship with his sister. She'd come to talk about the theater. Yet she couldn't help but ask more questions.

"Did you and Dorothy ever talk?"

He shook his head. "She never came out here, and I never set foot in the theater." He took a sip of coffee and eyed her over the cup. "Least of all the night she died."

"I didn't—"

"Of course you did. That's why you're here. Since I'm Dorothy's last living relative and will inherit the theater."

"I am interested in the theater…"

He ignored her. "I have a motive for murder. That's a fact. But Saturday evening, I was an hour away from Blithedale. Then I came back home and spent the night here, as I always do."

"Can anyone confirm where you were?"

"A dozen people can confirm where I was in the evening. But once I came back to my cabin, only the deer and birds knew I was here."

Alice tried to change the subject away from the murder. "The theater—"

"Was I anywhere near it?" Beau shook his head. "Miles away. You want to know where I was on Saturday evening? It's no secret. I was at an Alcoholics Anonymous meeting. I go every week, at least once."

"You're in A.A.?"

"You sound surprised." He laughed, and it was a gentle, sad sound. "I guess good news travels much slower than bad. Everyone in Blithedale still knows me as the town drunk. But I've been going to A.A. for more than half a year now."

"Did Dorothy know?"

He shrugged. "Maybe Mr. Gorny told her."

"Mr. Gorny? The theater's caretaker?"

"Sure," Beau said. "He drove me. In fact, he's driven me every time. He took me to my first meeting, encouraging me to start a new life. Believing in me when no one else believed in me."

He gazed into his coffee cup and frowned.

"I wonder what he'll think about me inheriting the theater, though…"

Alice cleared her throat. "Uh, yes. About that. What do you know about running a theater?"

Beau shook his head. "Nothing. Absolutely nothing."

CHAPTER 6

id-morning, Mr. and Mrs. Oriel stopped by Wonderland Books.

Since getting back to her store, Alice had been driving herself crazy imagining 50 ways Beau Bowers could ruin the Blithedale Theater. She'd just gotten to the 50th way that Beau could cause a disaster: by turning out to be the killer and getting locked up for life. What would happen to the theater then?

So her relief at seeing the couple—and being distracted— was so huge she almost hugged them.

The Oriels were a retired couple who'd recently bought a home in Blithedale. The remarkable thing about them was that they almost looked identical. They nearly always wore gray or beige or other muted colors—sea-foam green sweaters today—and the same thick-rimmed glasses. But even their faces looked similar, and Alice wondered whether so many years of marriage had somehow made them morph into duplicates of each other.

"Do you have any Ellis Peters mysteries?" Mrs. Oriel asked.

"Brother Cadfael," Mr. Oriel said.

And Mrs. Oriel added, "The medieval monk."

Alice smiled. The couple often completed each other's sentences. She said, "I have most of them as used paperbacks, if you don't mind a cracked spine."

Mrs. Oriel chuckled devilishly. "I don't, especially when it's the cracked spine of a corpse."

Alice winced, remembering the batten that had fallen on Dorothy. Not to mention Vince Malone, who'd fallen off scaffolding to his death. Puns about murder had taken on a new meaning since she'd moved to Blithedale.

"We're reading the entire Brother Cadfael series together," Mr. Oriel said, as Alice led them to the shelves. "So if you have a second copy of each, we'll take it."

Fortunately, Alice did have duplicates of books 1 through 5, and after gathering them, she rang them up. She enjoyed an image in her mind of Mr. and Mrs. Oriel snugly tucked into bed, both reading the same Brother Cadfael mystery and occasionally chuckling or comparing notes on suspects.

"And did you hear about the murder?" Mrs. Oriel asked.

Alice nodded. "Did you know Dorothy Bowers?"

"When we first came here years ago, we went to the theater a few times. The old Mr. and Mrs. Bowers were still alive then."

"That woman, Sandy Spiegel, invited us to *The Wizard of Oz* singalong," Mrs. Oriel said. "But sadly, it was canceled."

"Sadly, yes," Mr. Oriel echoed. "Still, we're happy to spend the evening reading our books."

"Very happy."

Mrs. Oriel gave her husband a warm smile, and he reciprocated. Alice was musing on what a wonder it was to meet couples who'd been married for decade, after decade, after decade, yet still showed such love and affection for each other. It was like witnessing a natural phenomenon that seemingly defied scientific explanation—a little like magic.

Her musing was interrupted, however, when Chief Jimbo stepped into the bookstore. The Oriels got their bag of books and said, "Toodle-oo," on their way out.

"How can I help you, Chief Jimbo?"

The chief of police smiled. The smile on his young face suggested he was unusually pleased with himself. "It's not you who can help me. Not this time."

He drew himself up to his full height and pulled up his sagging uniform pants.

"I've solved the case."

"You've what?" Alice leaned across the counter, certain she'd misheard him. "You solved Dorothy's death?"

"Her murder," he corrected her.

"Wait, did you just call her death a *murder*?"

Chief Jimbo looked even more self-satisfied. "That's right. Obviously, it was a murder. That steel bar—that batten— couldn't fall by itself."

Alice had a bad feeling. Her gut twisted. She hardly dared ask the question on her mind. She said, "Chief Jimbo, you don't think Beau did it, do you…?"

"Beau?" Chief Jimbo laughed. "Of course not."

A great weight lifted from her shoulders, and she exhaled. This was the best news she'd gotten all day. She smiled at Chief Jimbo. "What were you saying about that batten?"

"Forget the batten. I'm interested in the shoes. Obviously, the glittery red sneakers were a sign."

"A message," she said, nodding.

He held up a lecturing finger. "A signature."

"All right…" Not in a million years would she have expected Chief Jimbo to admit Dorothy was murdered, let alone agree with her about the key clues. "If the red sneakers—"

"The ruby-red slippers. Like in *The Wizard of Oz*."

"Right. You're saying the ruby-red sneakers are the killer's signature?" Alice frowned. "But that means…"

"That the killer has done it before."

He dug into one of his pockets and brought out a printout from an online site called *Serial Killers Galore*. He slapped the paper down on the counter, making Alice's pen holder jump, the pen's inside rattling. The printout showed a newspaper clipping from 15 years ago. The headline said,

"Another Dorothy Murdered—the Oz Killer Strikes Again!"

Alice looked up at Chief Jimbo, who was beaming with pride. "It's the Oz Killer," he said. "He's back!"

CHAPTER 7

*C*hief Jimbo left Alice in a confused state bordering on panic.

What could be worse than Beau Bowers killing his sister? A serial killer on the loose.

Mayor MacDonald's bleak vision of the press descending on Blithedale like a flock of vultures began to look downright cheery. If a serial killer was terrorizing town, it would be national—no, international—news. The FBI would shut down half the town. True crime enthusiasts would turn cheerful Blithedale into a twisted tourist destination, bringing busloads of conspiracy theories and leaving with morbid mementos.

Forget her worries about Beau ruining the Blithedale Theater. The future of the town itself might be at stake.

She needed fresh air. A walk in the woods. But instead, the rest of the day turned out to be busy. Lots of people came to buy books, the tiny house filling to capacity as people dropped in after work.

The notion of a bookshop in Blithedale was still a novelty,

and many locals visited the store simply to enjoy the irresistible pleasure of browsing. Inevitably, most couldn't resist taking a book or two home. That was good news for her business. But coupled with the stress of Chief Jimbo's news, it left her frazzled.

By the time she put up the "Sorry, We're Closed" sign, Alice's feet and back ached, and her brain was one big, throbbing headache.

Where she'd avoided her friends before, Alice now desperately wanted to see them. She needed their distraction. She needed their reassurance. But Ona had to deal with a couple of late arrivals to the inn and Becca was busy serving dinner, so Alice sat alone at the diner, eating a Cobb salad and distracting herself by studying the framed illustrations on the walls.

Each print came from a Dickens novel. The illustration hanging on the wall by her booth depicted a scene from a theater. The view showed the audience—a sea of happy, smiling faces. Except for one young man at the edge of the drawing. He stood apart from all the others, leaning against a wall or pillar and gazing miserably up at a balcony, presumably at his unrequited love. The caption read, "Mr. Guppy's desolation."

It didn't make her feel any better about herself.

Eventually, she gave up battling her thoughts, and faced them head on.

All right. So what do we actually know about Dorothy's death?

She speared another piece of lettuce and chewed it, as she considered the facts.

Dorothy Bowers, owner of the Blithedale Theater, had been struck down on stage sometime during the night between Saturday and Sunday. Because the theater was closed on Sunday, it wasn't until Alice and Ona came looking for her that the body was discovered. Which said something about the life Dorothy led. No partner. No friends.

No one had missed her for nearly 24 hours.

How sad, Alice thought. *I hope that never happens to me.*

Beau, her brother, last of the Bowers, would inherit the theater. He seemed horrified that the theater had become his burden. Hardly the sign of a man who wanted to murder his sister to inherit the family business. Anyway, if Chief Jimbo was right, then Beau had nothing to do with Dorothy's death —the infamous Oz Killer did.

But who was the Oz Killer? She dug out her phone and spent half an hour searching the Internet. There were references to the Oz Killer on forums devoted to serial killer lore. Yet as she read through the posts, there seemed to be disagreement about whether the Oz Killer could be considered a true serial killer.

The prime suspect, a man named Arthur Crumpit, had lived near Blithedale. Apparently, he'd killed a woman named Dorothy, blaming her for both his unrequited love and his dead mother's cruelty. It sounded psychotic. His mother's name had been Dorothy, and Crumpit was obsessed with *The Wizard of Oz*. The police never caught Crumpit, which only whipped the media into a greater frenzy. And when another murder happened across the country that bore striking resemblance to the first one, the newspapers quickly concluded that the Oz Killer had struck again.

All this she learned from forum posts published by people who seemed so sure of their theories—several referred to them as "facts." No one cited sources or provided links to newspaper articles.

Alice couldn't find more information than that. One person claimed to have identified Arthur Crumpit as living in Mexico under an assumed identity. Another said that he was a dentist, who'd killed the second victim during an operation. Several posts on a forum devoted to true crime and serial killers cast doubt on whether the second murder, in fact, had any connection to the first. By the time Alice was done reading, her idea of the case was more muddled than before.

She decided to put away her phone and give the Internet theorists a break. In the morning, she would visit the public library instead.

She got Susan's attention and treated herself to a slice of warm apple pie with a scoop of vanilla ice cream. For a moment, as the crunchy crust crackled between her teeth and mixed with the sweet vanilla ice cream and fruit, she wondered whether she'd be better off forgetting about the murder case. She toyed with the idea of trusting Chief Jimbo. Maybe he was right. After all, the killer's signature did match that of the Oz Killer. And that meant any day now, the FBI would get involved. Maybe she should focus her energy on bookselling…

After dessert, she went to the restroom, and as she came out, she overheard Becca, who was standing behind the counter, talking on the phone.

"She was here a minute ago, Ona. I'm sure you'll see her back at the inn soon." She paused, evidently listening to Ona, and Alice crept back a little, not wanting Becca to see her. "Yeah, I heard she went to Beau's, too. Andrea was out hiking and saw her. I agree—we should talk to her about it…"

Becca hung up and ducked down to get something from a fridge. Alice crept past the counter, then hurried to the door.

She wandered down Main Street, feeling conflicted. Now Becca and Ona were keeping tabs on her. She sighed. Of course, she understood that they wanted to help. They were her friends. But shouldn't friends also trust each other?

She didn't want to sneak around. But she also didn't want

Becca and Ona to corner her and force her to share what she'd learned—not yet. After all, she didn't know much yet.

It was getting dark. The street lamps cast a dim light on the sidewalk as she sauntered home. A bicyclist drifted past. Two women, arm in arm, passed her and smiled, wishing her a goodnight. On a beautiful night like this, it was impossible to imagine a murder could've been committed at the theater.

Back at the Pemberley Inn, Alice waited outside the glass-paneled doors, peeking inside. Ona was at the reception desk, working on the computer. Alice waited. Finally, Ona left the desk to see to something, and Alice slipped off her sneakers and carefully opened the front door.

She tip-toed up the stairs in her socks, but the step by Mr. Knightley creaked.

"Alice?" Ona said from below.

Alice took another step. No creak. Then another. Outside her door, she set down her sneakers at the foot of the Colonel Brandon mannequin. Then unlocked the door and let herself into her room.

Safely ensconced in the canopy bed, she turned off the lights and told herself to go to sleep. She lay in the dark, antsy with guilt and worry. She felt that if she tried to fix the Blithedale Theater problems, her friends would criticize her for not including them. But they didn't understand—the whole point was that she'd made the mess and she needed to fix it.

Before something even worse happens to the theater—or even to all of Blithedale.

She turned over and pressed her face into the pillow, promising herself, *The professionals will handle the murder. You just need to focus on Beau and the Blithedale Theater...and selling books.*

She tossed and turned that night, and only fell into a deep sleep toward morning. Then, when the hazy light of dawn peeked through the curtains, she half-woke from a strange dream. Was that a sound she'd heard outside her door? As if someone was creeping around? She closed her eyes again and turned over.

Just a dream...

CHAPTER 8

*I*n the morning, Alice planned to sneak out of the inn. But after getting ready, she stepped into the hallway. She stopped. The floorboards under the Colonel Brandon mannequin were bare. She swiveled around herself, looking for her shoes.

They were gone.

In her socks, she wandered down the stairs. The reception was empty. She moved through the old Victorian house to the back room, which served as a den for reading and playing games. Its French doors opened onto the backyard.

Alice took off her socks and continued on bare feet.

"Morning," Ona said.

She was sawing through a plank of wood. Surrounding her was the village of tiny houses—all her creations, great and small, from Swiss-style chalets to miniature Nantucket-style cottages—which she built faster than she could sell. So the village grew, and grew, and grew.

Alice stared at her.

"Where are my shoes?"

"Your shoes?" Ona kept sawing. Finally, the board split in half, the two halves dropping with a thud. "What shoes?"

"You took them, didn't you? You snuck up to my door early this morning and absconded with my sneakers."

"You mean those sneakers?"

Ona gestured with her saw at the roof of one of her tiny houses. Alice looked up. Her sneakers, the laces tied, dangling down from a little chimney.

She put her hands on her hips and frowned. "Why'd you do that?"

"Why'd you lie to me? Why'd you tell me you were opening your bookstore when, in fact, you were visiting Beau?"

Alice dropped her arms and looked away, feeling a blush come on.

"Alice, this is a tiny town. I could see you'd left the bookstore unattended. Becca works at the epicenter of all gossip. All I had to do was ask her if someone knew where you'd gone, and sure enough, people had seen you head to Beau's place."

"I'm trying to set things right…"

"Fine," Ona said. "But why does that have to be done alone?"

Alice said nothing. How could she explain? Ona wasn't the recipient of a loan from the Blithedale Future Fund. She wasn't the one who'd stocked half her store with used books that had been donated by locals. She wasn't the one living rent-free at the Pemberley Inn.

Ona sighed and put down the saw.

"Anyway, we can eat breakfast together, can't we?"

Alice nodded. "I never said we couldn't."

She wished she didn't sound so defensive. She didn't mean to. She tried to soften her voice. "Sorry, I need coffee."

"Then I say you and I go to the diner and drink a gallon of coffee."

That sounded good to Alice.

Ona retrieved Alice's sneakers, and 10 minutes later, they were seated at the counter at the What the Dickens Diner. They drained three cups each and ate a pile of pancakes, while listening to Becca tell them the latest gossip, and Alice began to feel better.

The latest gossip included rumors about Beau Bowers—some more believable than others. He'd stopped drinking (Alice could confirm that). He would be the new owner of the Blithedale Theater (yes, since no one else would inherit). He'd been attending community college to earn a degree in business administration and was planning to turn the theater into a night club (obviously untrue…Alice hoped).

"I don't believe that last one, either," Becca said. "But in every pile of rotten rumor, there may be a grain of truth."

Ona laughed. "I'm pretty sure Charles Dickens didn't say that."

"No." Becca winked. "But Becca Frye did."

By now, Becca had heard about Chief Jimbo's break-through in the case, too. In fact, he seemed to have told the entire town, proud that he was making progress. Alice told them what she'd learned about the Oz Killer.

"The Internet is full of theories masquerading as facts," Alice said. "But the public library should have more information."

"Great," Ona said. "After breakfast, we'll go to the library."

Alice didn't have the heart to argue. Besides, this wasn't theater business, as such—it was curiosity about the murder case. Which she had nothing to do with.

So, after they'd finished the last morsel of pancake, Alice and Ona headed to the public library.

It was a small, one-story brick building. Paint was peeling

off the window frames, and inside, the carpeting was worn down to the concrete. Despite the wear and tear, and obvious lack of resources, the library was cozy and decorated with colorful posters and mobiles dangling from the ceiling.

"This place could use a makeover," Alice said.

Ona nodded. "Add them to the Future Fund's list."

Alice winced inwardly, and glanced at Ona. Had there been judgement in Ona's comment? A reference to Alice ignoring any such list and going straight to Dorothy?

But Ona was a straight talker, and besides, she seemed entirely focused on the business at hand. She headed straight for the circulation desk, and Alice followed.

Behind the desk, a librarian stood at a standing desk, busily typing on her computer. She was also busy dancing. She had a pair of big headphones on and moved to the music, bopping her head and shaking her hips and mouthing the words.

Ona cleared her throat.

The woman jumped. She gave them a startled, deer-in-headlights look, and then scrambled to get the headphones off her head and fumbled with her phone, trying to switch it off. But taking off her headphones disconnected them, and for an instant, her phone's tinny speakers played the doo-wopper rock 'n' roll of the *Grease* soundtrack.

"Gosh," the woman said, straightening her clothes. She wore a name tag that said, *Lorraine Maxwell, Head Librarian.* "Sorry about that. Oh, you're the owner of the new bookstore. I came to the grand opening—what a delightful place."

"Thank you," Alice said.

"How may I help you?"

Alice introduced herself and explained their errand—that they were looking for more information about a murderer called the "Oz Killer."

"Goodness gracious," Lorraine said. "This has nothing to do with poor Dorothy's death, does it?"

Alice and Ona exchanged a look. Lorraine leaned over the counter and whispered, "Mum's the word. I won't tell a soul. We librarians know how to keep secrets. Now, come along, and I'll show you how to use our system to search for the Oz Killer."

Five minutes later, having listened attentively to Lorraine's instructions, Alice and Ona sat at a computer near the circulation desk. Lorraine stood over them, clearly interested. They'd already found a dozen digitized newspaper articles describing the murder of the first Dorothy. But each article sounded almost identical.

"They no doubt copied the Associated Press article," Lorraine explained. "See? The wording is strikingly similar."

There was no doubt about it. Each article rehashed the same information, often verbatim. A woman named Dorothy Smith had been murdered near Blithedale, her head bashed in with a blunt object. She'd been left wearing "sparkling shoes like the ones little Dorothy famously wore in *The Wizard of Oz*." There was a lot of speculation about the Oz Killer, including the information that the police had found a suspect. A young man named Arthur Crumpit, who had a brief relationship with Dorothy Smith as well as an obsession with the L. Frank Baum Oz books. Judging from the news, Arthur Crumpit was never caught.

Reports on the second murder, much later, echoed the first. The woman's name was Dorothy Johnson, and neighbors found her wearing a pair of "ruby-red sneakers, apparently a tribute to *The Wizard of Oz*." The killer had poisoned this Dorothy, not bludgeoned her, though that didn't stop the newspapers from stoking up fears that the Oz Killer had returned.

Alice and Ona continued to search through articles. But they found nothing else.

"Try searching for Dorothy Smith," Ona suggested.

Alice typed in the first victim's name, a few details about her, plus "Blithedale," to narrow the results.

"All the same articles. She only ever got mentioned in the news because of her murder."

"Now try the other one."

"Dorothy Johnson? Let's see…"

She added Johnson's hometown and state—halfway across the country—to narrow the results. A number of results popped up:

"Bingo Night at St. Martin's Church."

"Local Woman Wins a Prize for Floral Arrangement."

"A Thank You to This Year's Church Volunteers."

Alice scrolled down the long list of headlines.

"Wait," Ona said. "Look at that one."

"Dentist Arrested for Murder."

Alice clicked open the article. At her sides, she sensed Ona and Lorraine leaning closer to read as well. The story was disturbing. A dentist in Dorothy Johnson's town was arrested for poisoning his patients. He had offered appointments at odd times—late at night, at the crack of dawn—making it easier for him to remove the bodies afterward. He had confessed to killing three women, but the police were investigating him for the murder of a fourth woman, Dorothy Johnson, believed to be his first victim.

"Like the other victims, Dorothy lived alone, and initially, no one connected the dentist visit with her death," Alice said.

"So this dentist staged her death to look like the Oz Killer did it? But why?"

Alice shrugged. "Maybe to throw the cops off his scent?"

"That makes sense timing-wise," Lorraine said. "The Oz Killer would've still been in recent memory. Looks like he brought all his victims home and laid them on their couches, as if they'd simply fallen asleep. Only Dorothy got the Oz treatment."

Alice shuddered. "Creepy."

"Murder often is," Ona said.

Alice scanned the article again. Then looked at the ones mentioning the first murder. The more she considered it, the more she believed the murders were unrelated. The media would've been eager to continue the Oz Killer story, giving the murderous dentist an excellent opportunity to throw suspicion on the elusive Arthur Crumpit.

In fact, several articles described just how eager the press had been: The murders brought an army of journalists to the town, which then attracted outsiders wanting to see the scene of the crimes. Then disaster struck when a B movie producer made a horror film out of the ordeal. Fans of the horror film flocked to the town, staging tasteless reenactments and taking photos of the places the killer dentist had roamed. Whatever short-term business this unwanted attention brought, it wasn't much. And the negatives were far greater. One local newspaper described the ensuing mayhem as "the year our gentle town hardened." Property values plummeted. People moved away. The town sank into a depression—economic and spiritual.

Reading about the small town's fate, Alice shuddered. This could happen to Blithedale. Chief Jimbo wouldn't see the danger. He was proud to have worked out the connection between the Oz Killer and Dorothy's death. Soon, word would spread beyond Blithedale—then the journalists would descend on town, followed by the curious, and who knew what might happen, maybe a movie would be made about the Oz Killer, bringing the worst kind of attention to this beautiful town.

Alice exhaled. Someone would have to do something.

Starting with setting the record straight. She said, "Let's agree the Oz Killer didn't murder Dorothy Johnson. The dentist did it, copying the first murder. That would make Dorothy Smith the Oz Killer's first and only victim."

"Not much of a serial killer if you've only killed one person," Ona said.

"That's my point. If the dentist was a copycat, maybe the person who killed Dorothy Bowers is, too."

"You don't think the Oz Killer killed Dorothy Bowers? You think we're talking about three different murders?"

Alice shrugged. "That's my guess. But there's not much to go on, is there? Maybe there's a connection between Dorothy Smith and Dorothy Bowers we're missing. The newspaper articles provide almost no details on Dorothy Smith's murder. It's all so vague."

"Maybe the police withheld information," Ona suggested. Then, with a grin, she nudged Alice. "Hey, Nancy Drew, am I sensing you're *not* going to leave it to the professionals after all."

Lorraine looked up at Alice. "Oh, goodie. Are you going to do what you did with the Vince Malone murder?"

"I'm just going to get more information," Alice said, wishing she didn't sound so defensive. In fact, she was thinking Ona had hit the nail on the head: *With Blithedale's future at stake, I can't leave this to Chief Jimbo. I didn't think the murder was any of my business. But it is now.*

"Well, if you're looking for more details," Lorraine said cheerfully, "there is one person who might know a thing or two: Leonard Stout."

"The county coroner?"

"That's right. Lenny's been the county coroner for decades. I bet he remembers the case."

CHAPTER 9

*A*fter opening Wonderland Books for the day, Alice restocked shelves and then sorted through more boxes of donations, all the while thinking of nothing but the Oz Killer. Her absentmindedness cost her: She discovered that she'd shelved *The Complete Poems of Emily Dickinson* under E. And a copy of *Walden* sat next to Whitman's *Leaves of Grass*.

She was correcting her mistakes when a customer came into the store. An out-of-towner. The young man had coal-black hair and a face that seemed to be molded into a sneer.

"Can I help you find something?" Alice asked, putting Emily Dickinson where she belonged.

"I'm the one who does the finding. I'm Billy Brine."

"Nice to meet you, Billy Brine."

"I'm *the* Billy Brine." He lowered his voice from his high tenor to a baritone, apparently straining for bass. *"This is Billy Brine. And this...is...True Crime Truth."*

He smirked, waiting for Alice to react.

She shrugged. "Sorry, I don't know what that means—is it some kind of show?"

"Some kind of show?" Billy's eyes widened. "Are you kidding? My podcast is trending. It's in the top 5 of true crime podcasts." He repeated the name—*True Crime Truth*—and stared meaningfully at Alice, apparently expecting her to react. Having never heard of the podcast, she didn't dance with joy.

"That's, uh, great," Alice muttered.

In fact, worry balled up in her belly and tightened. Hopefully, it was a coincidence that a true crime podcaster had come to Blithedale.

"Were you looking for a specific book?"

Billy let out a quick breath, clearly exasperated by her reaction. "*The Wizard of Oz*. You got a copy of it?"

"Sure. In fact, I have the entire set of L. Frank Baum Oz novels." She went to the counter and pulled out the set she'd gotten as a donation. "They're in decent condition."

"It's a series?"

"Fourteen books."

"Nah, just gimme the first one. I need it for research."

The word research made the ball in her stomach tighten even more. Her worst fears were confirmed when Billy leaned against the counter and lowered his voice.

"I'm researching the Oz Killer."

Alice's voice caught in her throat. "The Oz Killer?"

"Yeah. Arthur Crumpit. He killed at least two women named Dorothy, and now it seems he's struck again."

"You see—" She swallowed. "—you see a connection between those murders?"

She rang up the hardback copy of *The Wonderful Wizard of Oz*.

Billy frowned. "Twenty bucks? For a book?"

"I have a paperback edition for $9.99."

"I'll take that instead."

Alice was glad not to separate the first book from the set.

At the back of her mind, she made a mental note to keep the 14-book set of Oz books together—some appreciative reader would adore finding the entire saga. She could tell this kid wasn't that person.

She found the paperback edition and rang it up, and Billy paid in cash.

"I can't divulge too much about my investigations," Billy said, picking up from where they'd left off. "But I can tell you I believe Crumpit is alive and well. Fact is, he's living in the Blithedale Woods."

"In the woods?" Alice couldn't hide her skepticism. "But why hide all these years, only to return now? And why target Dorothy Bowers?"

"You'll have to listen to my podcast to find out."

He grabbed the book off the counter. Just then, Mr. and Mrs. Oriel came into the store.

Billy reminded her, in that slightly deeper voice, "True Crime Truth."

Mrs. Oriel let out a little yelp. She covered her mouth with her hands.

"You're Billy Brine," she said. "I recognize your voice."

"The podcaster," Mr. Oriel said.

"True Crime Truth!" Mrs. Oriel exclaimed.

Billy smiled and straightened his posture, turning his jaw upward a little, as if preparing for a portrait.

"We love your podcast," Mrs. Oriel said. "Wait, are you are here to investigate Dorothy Bowers' death?"

"*I'm here in Blithedale,*" Billy said, having dropped his voice as deep as it would go, "*to unearth the truth about a brutal murder...a brutal murder that could only have been committed by a true monster: the Oz Killer.*"

Mr. and Mrs. Oriel exchanged eager smiles.

"You think a serial killer did it?" Mr. Oriel asked.

"I know he did," Billy said. "The evidence speaks for itself.

The Oz Killer is alive and well, living in the Blithedale Woods."

Mrs. Oriel gasped. Her husband put an arm around her.

Alice said, "Don't worry, Mr. and Mrs. Oriel. Chief Jimbo is still investigating. We don't actually know for a fact who killed Dorothy yet."

"But the Oz Killer…" Mrs. Oriel said.

"There's no evidence he's living in the Blithedale Woods," Alice insisted.

"Except there is. Tell them, sweetie."

Mr. Oriel nodded. "Someone broke into our new home and stole food, and we saw him run off…"

"A wild-looking man," Mrs. Oriel added. "Beau Bowers says he's spotted him, too."

"A giant, wild-looking man," Mr. Oriel continued, "all shaggy and bearded, like he's been living in the woods for some time."

"It could be the Oz Killer, couldn't it?"

Mrs. Oriel's question was directed at Billy.

Billy nodded. "Absolutely. I'll bet a hundred bucks that was Arthur Crumpit, the Oz Killer. He's back."

"What do you think, Alice?" Mr. Oriel asked.

A minute ago, Alice would've bet a hundred bucks that Billy's theory was wrong. But her gut, which had clenched itself into a tiny nut, felt otherwise. She didn't doubt the Oriels. They might be eccentric, in their own charming way, but they weren't prone to hallucinations or tall tales. If they saw a wild man running from their home, she believed them.

She bit her lower lip, thinking.

But who was this wild man? Could it really be Arthur Crumpit? Was it possible that Crumpit had been hiding in the vast forest—for more than a decade—waiting for the opportunity to strike again? Whether or not it was true didn't matter. Not if thousands—maybe millions—of people learned about it and descended on Blithedale to morbidly experience firsthand where the Oz Killer lived.

"I don't know…" she muttered, feeling sick to her stomach.

"You will soon," Billy said. "When I solve this murder case, the whole world will know."

CHAPTER 10

*T*he town was abuzz with excitement. Nearly every customer that came into the bookstore asked Alice if she'd heard that Billy Brine—*the* Billy Brine—had come to Blithedale. More than one person mentioned the news that someone had broken into the Oriels' home and that a wild-looking man had been seen running away. Surely, this was no coincidence. Surely, it was the killer.

Among her visitors was Chief Jimbo, who was unusually animated.

"Alice, you won't believe," he said breathlessly, "how close I am to solving the case, and now I even have a famous podcaster teaming up with me. He says he's going to help me organize a search. We're going to find this killer."

Alice couldn't speak. She simply nodded, all the while thinking this was the worst thing that could've happened. Billy would broadcast the investigation to the entire world. And now Jimbo had teamed up with him? If she didn't find the real killer, and fast, this would end in disaster for the entire town.

She needed to talk to the county coroner, Lenny Stout.

But how would she find him? She'd have to ask Becca or Susan at the diner—they knew everyone in town.

After another long day, she locked up her tiny house bookshop and headed down the street to the What the Dickens Diner.

Susan, in the waitress apron, greeted her with a smile and told her to find a seat and she'd be right with her. Alice put a hand on her arm to stop her before she could rush off.

"Susan, do you have any idea where Lenny Stout lives?"

"Oh, he lives outside Blithedale. A good hour's drive away."

Alice sighed. Not owning a car made everything more complicated.

"But why do you want to visit him at home," Susan said, "when you can talk to him right here?"

She gestured across the diner, and then excused herself.

Alice scanned the tables, the seats at the counter, and the booths. The restaurant was hopping. It seemed all of Blithedale was there, no doubt as hungry for gossip as for Becca's famous meatloaf and mashed potatoes. Alice even spotted unfamiliar faces, and worried this might be the first sign of outsiders coming to ogle the "crime town."

Becca rushed past, giving her a harried hello as she balanced two plates on each arm on her way to a booth near the back. The booth was packed with people, three on each leatherette seat. Other booths were similarly crammed.

Then Alice recognized the rumpled suit.

Lenny Stout sat alone in a booth, bent over a book while eating his meatloaf dinner. He'd scoop up a forkful of mashed potatoes and slowly guide it into his mouth, his eyes staying on the pages of his book.

She headed his way, thanking her lucky stars for bumping into him.

"You're Lenny Stout, the county coroner."

He looked up with a pair of sad eyes. "Thanks for noticin' me." He cocked his head. "And I remember you. You're Alice Hartford of Wonderland Books fame."

"Do you mind if I join you?"

He shrugged. "Nowhere else to sit."

She slid into the booth, sitting opposite him. He put aside his book, which, she noticed, was a battered copy of A. A. Milne's autobiography. She hadn't read it, and apart from knowing that Milne had written the Winnie-the-Pooh books, she knew nothing about him.

"Good book?" she asked.

"Familiar," he said. "I've read it before."

"Then it must be good."

"Who can tell? If something's so familiar, how do you know if it's good or bad?" He sighed. "I suppose it's as good as it gets."

She pretended to study the menu, which she already knew by heart. Lenny cut his meatloaf into small bite-sized chunks, then fed them into his mouth with a slow, almost mechanical regularity. She wondered if he even tasted the food.

She said, "Did you hear about Billy Brine coming to town?"

"*The* Billy Brine. Has anyone *not* heard?"

"Do you think there's any truth to what he says about the Oz Killer being back?"

Lenny said nothing. He divided his pile of mashed potatoes into sections, neatly divvying it into quadrants, like an urban planner designing city blocks.

Alice tried again. "The Oz Killer murdered a woman near Blithedale. Dorothy Smith. You worked as the county coroner back then, didn't you?"

Again, Lenny said nothing. Having finished his meatloaf, he scooped up the quadrants of mashed potato, eating each bite with a near-forensic meticulousness. After that, he ate his peas, one at a time.

"Do you see any similarities between the murders?"

Lenny finished his peas. His plate was clean. He took a sip of water. Then raised his napkin from his lap and dabbed at his mouth, then folded it and laid it next to his plate.

Finally, he laid a 10-dollar bill on the table and got up.

Before he left, however, he turned back to Alice and said, "You're not the first to ask me about the Dorothy Smith murder. Nor will you be the last." He sighed heavily. "I'm not complaining, but there it is."

"But the Oz Killer didn't do it," she said. "If people continue to believe that he did, Blithedale may be overrun with journalists and true-crime tourists. It could be a disaster." She held out a hand, gesturing for him to sit down again. "Please."

He shook his head, looking sad. Then turned and shuffled off toward the exit.

As Alice watched him go, Becca came to her booth and cleared away Lenny's plate and water glass.

"Any luck getting information out of Lenny?"

"No, and I don't see that anyone else has enough information about this case to make any sense of it."

"You'll find a way." Becca winked at her. "Maybe take another look at the Bowers family. After all, most murders turn out to be committed by someone close to the victim."

Becca was right. Alice should've thought of that, too—if the Oz Killer suggested an outsider killed Dorothy, the truth probably lay closer to home. She'd have to talk to Beau again.

CHAPTER 11

*T*he next morning, Alice got lucky. Shortly after opening Wonderland Books, Beau Bowers stepped inside. He spun around himself, naked wonder on his face.

"Wow, I can't believe how many books you've packed into this tiny space."

"You've got a few of your own in that cabin of yours."

"And I'd like to get more." Beau slid a paperback off a shelf—a copy of Richard Powers' *The Overstory*—and read the blurb on the back. "This one sounds fascinating." He moved to the next shelf and grabbed another book, *Death in Holy Orders* by P.D. James. "And this one, too." He caught sight of another title—*After She's Gone* by Camilla Grebe—and grabbed that. "Oh, I've been meaning to read this for years."

In a matter of minutes, Beau's arms were laden with books. He put them down on the counter with a thunk and stared at the big pile. He sighed.

"It's too much—I'd better pick and choose," he said, beginning to sort them into two piles—one with books to buy, the other to put back on the shelves. "When I get the inheritance, I guess I can buy a lot more books. And Dorothy has books at her place, too."

"Was she a big reader?"

He shrugged. "She's got a couple of bookshelves at home. Mostly old stuff—Sarah Orne Jewett, O. Henry, and some plays by Eugene O'Neill—and then books on business and music. She loved music. Her house has wall-to-wall shelves in one room, and it's crammed with vinyl records and CDs. Everything from jazz and classical to bluegrass and rock 'n' roll."

He studied his two piles of books and frowned. Then he moved a book from the "put back" pile to the "buy" pile. Alice could relate. Whenever she divided books into two piles— the ones to keep and the ones to cut—she invariably gave last-minute pardons to most of the ones in the cut pile.

Beau said, "Truth is, I haven't had time to go through all her stuff. It's overwhelming. I'm going there now. I'll take a look around and get a sense of what I'll keep and what I'll get rid of."

"You're not moving into her house?"

He shook his head. "I'll sell the house. That was our parents' home, and it's too full of memories. I'm happy living in my cabin. I like small, cozy spaces." Then he smiled. "Though I would love to put in a better kitchen. Oh, a full bathroom. The outhouse and cold showers are rustic and quaint in summer, but not much fun in winter."

"You should talk to Ona. She's got beautiful tiny houses in the style of log cabins."

"Great idea. I'll go talk to her after I check out Dorothy's stuff. And then head to the diner for lunch." He looked down at his feet, shy all of a sudden. "I'm actually enjoying spending time in town and seeing people…"

He paid for his books, looking at each one again, as excited as a kid who's gotten a new toy.

Alice smiled, increasingly feeling a connection with Beau. He was a friendly, kind-hearted man, who deserved a second chance. Still, he could be a disaster for the theater, if he didn't get the right help.

"You know, there's this thing we call the Blithedale Future Fund…"

Beau's eyes widened. "I know that name. Dorothy left a whole folder full of documents, and it's marked 'Blithedale Future Fund.' In fact, it's among the papers I was planning on throwing away, since her work stuff is all at the office."

Alice nearly gasped. "No, don't throw it away. What if the papers contain important information about how Dorothy wanted to run the theater?"

"Mr. Gorny's helping me—he's encouraging me to develop my own vision and go my own way."

"That's great, but—"

"Better to toss the old papers and start with a clean slate."

"But—but—"

"I'd better go. I have a meeting with Mr. Gorny later."

Before she could get the words out, he'd grabbed his books and headed out. Alice went to the doorway and watched him walk down Main Street, his stiff gait reminding her—once again—of the Tin Woodman. In *The Wizard of Oz*, the Tin Woodman wanted a heart. Beau didn't seem to lack one, though the question was whether he had the brains to run the Blithedale Theater.

Dorothy's plans for the Blithedale Future Fund might contain vital information. She'd run the theater for many years. That knowledge couldn't be lost. And if Becca was right about the murderer being someone closer to home, maybe Dorothy's presentation could provide clues to the killer, too.

In either case, Alice needed to get her hands on that folder before Beau threw it out.

What was it Becca was always saying—that quote by Dickens? "The most important thing in life is to stop saying 'I wish' and start saying 'I will.' "

She locked up and put the "Be Back Soon" sign on the front door. Then dug out her phone, thinking she'd call Ona and get her help. She stopped herself.

She put away her phone.

That's right. I can handle this on my own.

CHAPTER 12

*D*orothy's home was a two-story clapboard house with a shingled roof. Everything painted white. Purple flowers in window boxes. A purple front door.

Guess I know what Dorothy's favorite color was...

Like many homes in Blithedale, Dorothy's was surrounded by forest. Trees rose on all sides of the house, except the front facing the street. That was good. It shielded the house from its neighbors and made Alice's job of hiding easier.

Occasionally, she glimpsed Beau as he passed a window. He opened the ones on the ground floor. Probably to air out. He stood in front of the living room windows for a while, staring out, scratching the back of his neck, looking to Alice like he was overwhelmed. Then he disappeared again.

A few minutes later, he shut the windows again. He came out of the front door and locked it behind him, stopping at a trash can in the driveway to dump a stack of papers. Then he hurried down the street, hands shoved in his pockets.

She waited. Since he'd mentioned a meeting with Mr.

Gorny, she was sure he wouldn't suddenly return. Pretty sure, anyway.

When she felt confident Beau wasn't coming back, Alice stepped out of her hiding place and crossed the street. She tried to look casual, as if she belonged. As casual as one can look rooting around in someone else's garbage.

She dug her hand into the trash can and came up with a handful of papers. Old electricity bills. Invitations to renew magazine subscriptions (*Rolling Stone*, *JazzTimes*, and others). Requests to donate to a political candidate. Nothing interesting. Alice dug out the rest of the papers. A letter from an insurance company introducing a change to Dorothy's homeowner policy. More requests to donate to a political candidate—a different one. And finally, decade-old bank statements. Nothing at all.

With a sigh, Alice dropped them back into the trash. Any hopes of finding Dorothy's presentation went with them. She'd have to look inside the house.

She didn't bother trying the front door. She knew it was locked. Instead, she headed around the house to the backyard.

The yard was small; the lawn sloped downward for only about 20 yards before trees swallowed it. Nothing back here. No garden furniture, no gazebo, no sense of Dorothy using the yard for any extracurricular activities. That fit with what she'd learned about Dorothy—all work and no play.

There was a wooden deck rising to ground floor level, exposing the concrete basement's outer walls below. The deck was as empty as the lawn. She climbed the steps and came to a screen door. She pulled the handle. The door was locked.

Looking around, however, she caught sight of a window that stood ajar. Beau must've forgotten to close it. She was sure she could push it open and climb in—if she could reach it.

The window was on the ground floor, but the distance to the lawn below made it inaccessible. Her only chance was to stand on the deck railing and stretch out a hand to grab the windowsill.

She took a deep breath and tried to think positive thoughts.

Easy peasy…you've climbed stuff before.

She climbed the railing, careful to maintain her balance. Then, crouching, she reached out. Her fingers touched the windowsill. She tried to grasp the windowsill. Too far. But the tips of her fingers caught the edge, and she eased it open.

The window was now wide open. But a considerable distance separated her from the sill.

No way I'm jumping…

But she didn't see any other way.

She took a deep breath. She tensed her thigh muscles, getting ready to spring.

One…two…three…

She jumped. She hit the windowsill with her belly, whacking the air out of her, and then began to fall. Sliding down, she scrambled to get a grip and, at the last instant, caught hold of the windowsill. She clung to it, her legs dangling down, and she cursed herself for this stupid idea.

The idea that you can pull yourself up is even stupider…

Again, though, she didn't see any other way.

She used all her strength. Hoisting herself up, she grunted, cursed, and rising, rising, rising, finally threw an elbow over the windowsill. Then another.

You can do it…

She let out a grunt. With a final heave-ho, she pulled herself up and wriggled her belly across the threshold. She fell to the floor on the other side with a painful bump and knocked something over with a clatter.

For a moment, she lay still, panting.

After a while, she got to her knees, her back aching, and she stood up. She'd knocked over a lamp on a bedside table. Fortunately, it wasn't broken. She put it back in its place. Then looked out the window. She leaned out to survey her accomplishment, congratulating herself.

That was a tough jump and one heck of a climb.

She'd done well. She'd—

When she saw what lay below the deck, she cursed herself.

In the crawl space beneath the deck lay a ladder.

Disgusted with herself, she turned away from the window. She'd better get going, if she was going to get the most out of her clandestine visit.

She'd landed in what must be a guest room. The small room could only fit a single bed and a bureau and the small bedside table she'd bumped. She wondered how often Dorothy used this room. Did she ever have guests? Dorothy apparently had no real friends, and with no connection to her brother and her parents long dead, no Bowers relatives to socialize with.

Her phone pinged. She'd forgotten to silence it.

Digging it out of her pocket, she saw that Ona had messaged her:

WHERE R U?

She ignored the message, putting her phone on "Do Not Disturb." If she found what she came for, she could share it with Ona and Becca—and hopefully prove that she'd been right to identify the theater as an ideal business to support.

She wandered out into a hallway and into the living room.

Beau hadn't been kidding about Dorothy's interest in music. The wall-to-wall bookshelves consisted of more vinyl records and CDs than Alice had ever seen in one place before. In fact, it was a rare sight these days, given that most people relied on online streaming services. Though she had heard about music connoisseurs favoring vinyl and CDs over digital formats.

A bust of Beethoven adorned the mantelpiece above the brick fireplace. Framed posters on the walls depicted famous musicians—Nina Simone, Edith Piaf, and Bob Dylan—and on a low cabinet stood an impressive stereo with a turntable and CD player flanked by giant speakers.

On top of the stereo lay a jewel case for a CD. The cover showed Blithedale's own bluegrass trio, the Pointed Firs. Alice smiled. She herself loved the Pointed Firs' jaunty bluegrass tunes.

The living room opened onto a dining room, which was where she'd seen Beau stand and stare into the distance. An antique oak dining table dominated the space. It had heavy, carved legs. A couple of bookshelves against the walls contained the books Beau had mentioned, and in between them stood a hutch with vintage glassware.

Papers lay in piles on the dining table. Manila folders. Ring binders. It seemed Beau had pulled out Dorothy's paperwork and begun the long process of reviewing everything. No wonder he'd looked overwhelmed.

Alice moved around the table, flipping through the documents. Now, where was that presentation?

There were ring binders with taxes dating back two decades. Logs of every movie ever shown at the theater. Income. Expenses. Catalogs from film distributors, some of them yellowing with age.

Alice was examining a brochure from a company that bought and sold second-hand 35mm movie projectors when she heard a sound behind her. She spun around.

A bump. It had come from within the house.

She listened.

Was that a faint creaking?

She put down the brochure and crept into the living room. If Beau had come back, she'd need to get out—and fast. She backtracked, heading for the hallway and the guest room.

Halfway across the hallway toward the guest room, her heart jumped into her throat. She stopped.

The top of the ladder rested against the windowsill. It wobbled, creaking as someone out of sight climbed the rungs.

Alice stood rooted to the ground, even as her mind yelled at her.

Run. Hide. Get out. Anything. Just do it!

A pair of hands gripped the top of the ladder. Dirty hands. Then a head rose above the windowsill. Shaggy hair. A coarse, unruly beard. A pair of wild eyes. That got even wilder as they caught sight of her.

He dropped out of sight.

The ladder creaked and thumped against the outside wall as the wild man made his escape.

The sudden clatter broke Alice's paralysis, and she leaped forward. In a flash, she was at the window.

But the wild man was fast. He bolted across the lawn and into the trees, the hunter green jacket he wore blending with the foliage.

He crashed through bushes and past trees and then, as he wove into the tapestry of branches and leaves, he vanished. The woods grew quiet again.

But only for a moment.

A dog barked nearby. Someone called out, "Hey, who's there? Beau—is that you?"

A neighbor. Alice, panicking, threw herself over the windowsill.

She grabbed the ladder and scrambled down to the grass.

Where was the neighbor?

Hoping for the best, she backtracked. She ran around the house. As she reached the driveway, she glanced over her shoulder and caught sight of a man emerging from the woods with a dog on a leash.

She didn't stop. She kept running.

CHAPTER 13

*T*he next morning, Ona cornered her at the diner.

"Hey," she said, slipping onto the leatherette seat across from hers, "why are you ignoring my messages?"

"I'm not. I responded to you."

"Right—*after* you got back to Wonderland Books. Where were you before that?"

"Nowhere." Alice hid her face by drinking deeply from her coffee cup. "Out for a walk. Just having a look around."

Becca came by with a coffee pot and refilled Alice's cup and served Ona as well. Without meeting Alice's eyes, she said, "Someone yesterday took a look around Dorothy's home. A neighbor claims he saw the so-called wild man. Funny thing is—" She looked at Alice. "—he also thinks he saw a woman running from the house."

"Two burglars?" Ona said. "Dorothy's home must be full of treasures."

Becca, still watching Alice, said, "Enough treasures for Beau to protect them. He's paid a security company to install a system this morning."

Alice choked on her coffee. Becca slapped her on the back.

"He—" she spluttered. "—he did?"

Becca and Ona were staring at her. Alice grabbed a napkin and wiped coffee from her chin, trying to ignore their stares. Finally, she couldn't take it anymore.

"All right. I broke into Dorothy's home."

"I knew it!" Ona leaned forward. "Why? What did you find?"

Alice groaned. "I didn't find anything. I got interrupted by—"

"The wild man!" Lorraine Maxwell burst into the diner. "The wild man's broken in. He's robbed the public library!"

Alice, Becca, and Ona exchanged glances. Then abandoned their coffee cups and the pot on the table and hurried to Lorraine's side. Becca put an arm around the librarian, but she shook it off.

"He could be there now," she said.

One of truckers at the counter got out his cell phone and called Chief Jimbo.

"I can't go back there alone," Lorraine said. "But what if he's damaging the books and our computers and—"

"We'll come with you," Ona said. Then nudged Alice. "Won't we?"

Alice nodded.

"We're all coming," Becca said, loudly and gestured toward the other guests at the diner. Susan threw off her apron. Truckers slipped off their stools. Teenagers emerged from their booths. They filed out onto Main Street, leaving diner empty.

On the way down Main Street, backed by an exodus of townsfolk, Lorraine seemed to regain her composure and courage—and by the time they reached the public library, she'd turned from fearful to indignant.

"Look what that monster did," she said.

Someone had forced the door open, warping the metal frame.

"Looks like a crowbar," Ona said, studying the gouges in the door frame.

"As soon as I saw, I hurried over to the diner," Lorraine said. "I didn't even dare go inside."

"No alarm?"

Lorraine shook her head. "It stopped working years ago, and it was never a priority to have it fixed. We have so many other things that need fixing."

Inside the library, Alice expected to see chaos. Windows smashed. Books strewn across the floor and ripped to shreds. Computers missing. But it looked as peaceful as ever. The worst, it seemed, was that the burglar had left muddy boot prints on the carpeting.

While the truckers and teenagers and others fanned out to search the library for any signs of the intruder, Alice, Ona, and Becca helped Lorraine look for signs of theft.

During their search, Alice looked up and saw others engaged in the same job, and she was amazed: Everyone was patiently doing their part to make sure the library was OK. She would never have thought to enlist everyone's help in this way—Becca really was incredible.

Gradually, people returned from the recesses of the building with the same report: no sign of the burglar. And no sign of anything destroyed or, as far as they could tell, missing.

After a while, Lorraine herself said, sounding surprised, "They're right—nothing's missing."

"Nothing at all?" Alice asked.

"Well, it will take time to determine if any books are missing, of course. But if the burglar took a book or two, it would be no worse than many other patrons."

Most people had left the library to return to the diner. Becca and Susan said their goodbyes, needing to go back to work. The truckers interpreted this as final confirmation that their services were no longer required, and they trudged out the door, heading back to the diner to finish their lumberjack breakfasts.

Alice scanned the space, which was now, without half the town milling about, considerably less crowded. "What else could a person come here for, if not books?"

"Restroom?" Ona said.

"Or a place to hide, maybe. But then the woods are a much better place for that…"

Ona snapped her fingers. "Phones and computers."

Lorraine went behind the circulation desk. She touched the keyboard to her computer and the screen sprang to life.

"I'm sure I shut down my PC yesterday."

"What about the password?"

Lorraine, giving Alice and Ona a sheepish look, pointed to a sticky note on the side of the screen. It said, "PW: Sandy!" Alice wished she could feel superior to Lorraine, but she herself had a little notebook in which she kept all her passwords and pin codes, perfect for a thief wanting access to all her accounts.

Lorraine sat down and clicked her mouse, opening a browser.

"The phone is an Internet phone, so if the burglar made any calls, I can see them here…" As Alice and Ona moved behind the circulation desk to get a better view, Lorraine squinted at the screen. "Oh, my. He did. Three calls." She opened a separate browser window and typed in a search query, checking the numbers. "All calls to numbers in the city, including a newspaper."

"Let's call them and ask," Alice suggested.

Lorraine looked up at her. "Ask them what? Whether they got calls during the night from a burglar?"

"Exactly."

Despite her skepticism, Lorraine made the calls. The newspaper transferred her to a handful of people until finally she got hold of someone who could answer her questions.

"Yes, a burglar…from Blithedale…well, I don't know why he would call. That's why I'm calling to ask…no…and there's no way…? I see."

She hung up, shaking her head.

"They got lots of calls during the night, and nothing out of the ordinary. Usually, at that time, they're professional calls—often fact checking—or crazy people calling to share their conspiracy theories."

Alice and Ona exchanged a look. A wild man in the woods with crackpot conspiracy theories. It sounded like they might be dealing with an unhinged person.

"What about the other numbers?" Alice asked.

Lorraine made the first call, putting the speaker on so Alice and Ona could hear.

A man answered. After some back-and-forth, it emerged that he was a retired journalist. But once he understood why Lorraine was calling, he turned grumpy. Who had called him was none of her business. "If some idiot wakes me in the middle of the night to ask me questions, I don't think I need to tell you anything. Goodbye."

The journalist seemed to know something, but what? It didn't matter that Lorraine had mentioned the break-in might be related to a murder investigation. The grumpy old man clearly had no intention of talking.

Lorraine dialed the third and last number. She turned and gave Alice and Ona a surprised frown. Then put the phone on speaker.

"You've reached Winnemac Federal Correctional Institution. Please listen to the following options…"

Lorraine hung up.

"Why would he call a prison?"

Alice shrugged. "Calling his other burglar friends? Check the browser history. Maybe that will tell us something."

"It's a long shot," Lorraine said with a sigh, but she opened the history in the browser and scrolled down the list of websites. "All of these were searched during the night…"

She opened each web page.

"Whoa," Ona said.

Alice leaned closer, staring at the screen.

Nearly every web search query was for "Oz Killer" or "Arthur Crumpit" or some variation thereof. The results brought up pages with chat forums, newspaper articles, and videos featuring true crime enthusiasts talking about Arthur Crumpit and his mother issues. There was even an article about the murder at the Blithedale Theater.

But the burglar had run a search on another name, too, bringing up news articles, school records, and, of course, podcast episodes.

Alice and Ona looked at each other.

"Billy Brine…"

CHAPTER 14

The burglar wasn't the only one interested in Billy Brine.

Later that morning, Alice sold three books about podcasting. Two of the customers were truant teenagers, obviously more interested in an illustrious online career than in attending class, and the last was a middle-aged man who seemed as embarrassed as if he were the one skipping class.

"I've been toying with the idea," he said. "My wife is always telling me I need a hobby."

"You're going to start a podcast?"

He shrugged. "If a kid like Billy Brine can do it, maybe I can, too."

After the man left, Alice restocked her shelves. Provided she didn't confuse the books, it was a convenient time to reflect on what they'd learned at the library.

She didn't know this for a fact, but she was fairly sure the burglar and the wild man in the woods were the same person. He'd tried to break into the Oriels' place. He'd tried to get into Dorothy's. And now he'd entered the public library.

Where would he strike next?

It occurred to her to talk to Becca and Ona. But Lorraine's entrance had distracted them from their conversation. She hadn't fully explained why she'd broken into Dorothy's home, and she still felt reluctant to involve them. Whenever she seemed close to doing something that would prove her independence—her ability to do things without their support—they pulled her back in. It made her feel dependent on them, as if the only reason she had a life in Blithedale was because of their charity.

She sighed. She'd just have to work this out on her own.

So, why was the wild man in the woods interested in the Oz Killer? Interested enough that he'd risk breaking into the public library to access a phone and a computer?

The obvious answer: The wild man was the killer. He was obsessed with how his "handiwork" was being presented by the media. And that was why he was interested in Billy Brine, too—after all, Billy's podcast was going to feature the Oz Killer.

But if Billy hadn't released his podcast episode yet, how could the wild man know that? Half of Blithedale had heard that Billy was investigating the Oz Killer, but she doubted the wild man was hanging out at the diner, listening to the latest gossip.

Unless Billy had already announced his intentions…

Back at the counter, she opened her phone and found Billy's podcast. She checked the show notes. His latest episode focused on an unsolved crime from 30 years ago. The Oz Killer went unmentioned. But on social media, Billy had told the entire world about his latest obsession: "Heading to Blithedale to catch the infamous Oz Killer."

As she considered this, she noticed that one of his older episodes was called "The Killer's Return—why murderers go back to the scene of the crime."

This made her think, *If the wild man is the killer, and he broke in to the library, and tried to break into Dorothy's place, wouldn't he try the theater, too?*

She looked up a local number and dialed it.

"Mr. Gorny? This is Alice from Wonderland Books…"

CHAPTER 15

"*W*elcome," Mr. Gorny said, as he opened the front door to the theater.

She stepped inside the lobby and breathed in the lingering smell of popcorn. Once again, the happy memory of her mom giving her a coin for a gumball came back to her, and she couldn't keep from smiling.

"It's a special place," Mr. Gorny said, returning her smile.

He led her past the gumball machine and the vintage phone booth to the concession stand. She was happy to have a chance to visit again and learn more about the theater—not just as the scene of the crime, but also as a business that would contribute to Blithedale's future. Maybe Mr. Gorny could shed more light on Beau's ability to run that business.

"Can I offer you a drink?" he asked.

"No, thanks," Alice said. "I really came to check on whether there's been any sign of a break-in."

Mr. Gorny shook his head. "As I mentioned on the phone, I've noticed nothing. Not that it isn't possible, but since the weekend—" He shook his head sadly. "—Chief Jimbo and state forensics have been through here so many times, it's felt more like a train station than a movie theater."

"I don't see any crime scene tape."

"They took it down yesterday. Technically, we're allowed to open again. But that's not my decision. That's for Beau Bowers to decide."

"The FBI won't be involved?"

"Not yet." He grimaced. "Believe me, I've demanded a better investigation, but Lenny Stout says he consulted the state cops on the matter and they see no cause for making this anything but a local investigation."

That was interesting. It made Alice wonder once more what Lenny knew. Presumably something that confirmed that the Oz Killer didn't murder Dorothy—otherwise the state police or even the FBI would've taken over.

Now Beau would reopen. She wondered how he'd handle his first days on the job. It was clear he'd turned a corner in his life. But managing a business was a big step.

"What do you think of Beau managing the theater?"

"It's the right thing," Mr. Gorny said. "He's a Bowers, after all."

"But he hasn't always been—" She paused, looking for a delicate way of describing it. "—capable of running the business."

"He's sober now. He'll do fine."

"He says you helped him get sober."

"He said that?" Mr. Gorny chuckled. "He gives me too much credit. Only one person could make Beau sober, and that was Beau. I just gave him a ride to A.A meetings."

"Has he talked to you about what will happen to the theater? I understand Dorothy had plans to change things…"

Mr. Gorny looked surprised. "Why, he'll carry on the tradition, of course. That goes without saying. The Bowers have run this theater for generations. Plans to change things?" He shook his head. "Dorothy was a staunch defender of the family legacy, and so am I. Now that Beau is sober, he can take responsibility, as he should. He can develop his own vision for how the theater should be run…in line with family tradition, of course."

"But he hasn't started yet?"

"Well, he's visited the theater, and we've had conversations about how we do things around here. It hasn't been easy with an ongoing investigation, but now that the police are gone, he and I can get to work. I've taken the liberty to restock the fridges and clean. So we're ready to reopen."

The concession stand did look clean and tidy. The popcorn machine would need to be filled and turned on, of course, but it wasn't difficult to imagine the theater opening its doors to movie goers this weekend.

"Any chance I could take a look at the auditorium?"

"I don't see why not."

He led her through the lobby to the double doors that opened onto the only auditorium in the theater. Most movie theaters had more than one screen. The Blithedale Theater didn't. She could see how it would be difficult to compete with the multiplexes, where you got the latest blockbusters, plus you could pick and choose from a dozen options.

They wandered down the sloping aisle between the red-plush chairs. The raised stage ahead was bare. But in Alice's mind, she could see clearly where Dorothy's body had lain. Mr. Gorny must've been thinking along the same lines. He sighed.

"I still can't believe Dorothy's gone…"

"You knew her well."

"Better than most." He shook his head. "She had years ahead of her to continue her good work. Then that madman…"

He exhaled, leaving his sentence unfinished.

At the foot of the stage, she looked up into the fly space with its many metal bars and ropes and other rigging.

"If someone pulled the rope that held the batten that killed Dorothy, where would they need to stand?"

"Over there."

Mr. Gorny pointed into the wings.

From down here, the curtains would've concealed the killer. But Dorothy had been standing on stage, and she would've seen the person. The timing would have to be perfect. She'd have to stand in the exact spot for the metal bar with the lamps to hit her. Alice wondered about this. What were the chances that the killer could've gotten it right?

Unless Dorothy knew the person. Trusted the person.

She glanced over at Mr. Gorny, and considered him. He could've done it. He knew the rigging and Dorothy wouldn't have suspected anything if she'd seen him in the wings, handling the rope. But where was the motive? Mr. Gorny had dedicated his life to the theater and the Bowers family, and he spoke highly of Dorothy. Besides, like Lenny Stout, Mr. Gorny had been quick to dismiss Chief Jimbo's idea that Dorothy's death had been an accident, and he'd demanded a thorough investigation.

But since Mr. Gorny had known Dorothy better than anyone, he might know something about her enemies—if she had any.

"Did anything strange happen in the days before Dorothy's death?" Alice asked. "Or did she have any confrontations with people?"

Mr. Gorny shook his head. "It was business as usual. If anything, Dorothy was more energetic and enthusiastic than ever about the movie theater. She was truly passionate about this place."

He looked around, a smile on his face as he appreciated

the auditorium. Then, gradually, his eyebrows pressed together in a frown.

"Except…"

"Except what?"

"Well, there was the cancelation of *The Wizard of Oz* singalong. A fairly last-minute decision, because so few people signed up. Dorothy used a sign-up system to gauge interest, and only about half a dozen people signed up for that singalong. But lots of people expressed an interest in *Grease*." He tsk-tsked. "If you ask me, these singalongs are silly, anyway. Why can't people just sit quietly and enjoy the movie?"

"But was the cancelation something unusual?"

"It wasn't typical. But that wasn't what I was thinking of. I was thinking of the meeting Dorothy had with Sandy Spiegel on Friday. She's the woman who lobbied Dorothy to do *The Wizard of Oz* singalong. When she heard about the cancelation, she demanded a meeting."

"She was upset?"

Mr. Gorny gave a low whistle. "She was furious. She stomped out of Dorothy's office, yelling like a madwoman. I was getting the concession stand ready, and I could hear her through the door to the back stairwell."

"What did she say?"

Mr. Gorny chuckled. "You won't believe it. She said, 'You're a wicked witch, Dorothy. I hope you melt.'"

CHAPTER 16

*I*t was a good thing Alice returned to Wonderland Books after that, because the rest of Thursday proved busy, and by the time she was closing the store, dark clouds rolled over the Blithedale Woods. She'd hoped to visit Sandy Spiegel to ask her about *The Wizard of Oz* singalong. But a heavy downpour convinced her to stay indoors.

She spent the evening in the Pemberley Inn's lounge, curled up on an armchair, drinking mint tea, and reading a paperback edition of *Jane Austen's Letters*. Ona joined her, sitting on a nearby armchair, deeply engrossed in Lucy Worsley's *Jane Austen at Home*.

The rain pattered against the windowpanes. Ona's pages rustled as she turned them. Otherwise, no sounds intruded on them. It was the height of coziness, and it would've been perfect to sit in companionable silence, if it hadn't felt so awkward.

Alice tried to ignore the feeling. After all, Ona seemed to be enjoying herself. So why did Alice feel so uncomfortable? These days it was like she didn't feel comfortable in her own skin anymore.

She couldn't concentrate on her book. She kept thinking of Beau Bowers and the Blithedale Theater. She admired Mr. Gorny for how he was helping Beau. He'd helped many Bowers family members succeed, and yet times had changed. He didn't seem willing to change much. Could it be that his devotion to the theater and the family would actually harm it? If Beau couldn't bring the theater into the 21st century— for example, by upgrading to digital film—then how could it possibly survive in the long run?

She had no answers to those questions. They only fueled her worry.

In comparison, the mystery of who killed Dorothy Bowers, which was, of course, tied up with the fate of the theater, was nevertheless not as stressful to think about. There was an important connection between the singalong and the murder. She'd neglected that line of enquiry, and she looked forward to tomorrow when she could talk to Sandy Spiegel about it.

All night, it rained. But the next morning, Friday, the skies were blue, the sun so bright and cheerful that it seemed eager to please, and so were the people Alice greeted on her walk from the Pemberley Inn to the diner. Half the town stopped her to chat about the weather and the day ahead, including the Oriels, who had spent a cozy evening finishing the first Brother Cadfael mystery.

"What an interesting life," Mrs. Oriel said.

"The life of a monk," Mr. Oriel clarified.

"Yes, and the life of Ellis Peters."

"Hers, too," he agreed.

At the diner, Alice had breakfast at the counter—a bowl of overnight oats with strawberries and blueberries and a dollop of yogurt—and while Becca made coffee, she made chit-chat. At one point, she made a casual remark about "a woman named Sandy."

"Sandy Spiegel," Becca said. "What's up with Sandy?"

"Does she live in town?"

"No, out in the woods. Along the northbound road beyond the old camp. Why?"

"Oh, just curious."

Alice finished her breakfast and headed out, determine to hike to Sandy's place and get back before she needed to open the bookstore for the day. She was halfway up the northbound road when she heard the rumble of a vehicle coming up behind her.

A pickup truck passed her. Then pulled over to the shoulder.

Alice sighed. She recognized the truck.

Through the open window, Ona gave her one raised eyebrow. Her eye-patch glittered in the morning light.

"No discussion," she said. "Hop in."

They drove up the road and Ona didn't chide her for leaving her and Becca out. She simply said, "So, tell me how Sandy Spiegel's involved."

Alice explained what Mr. Gorny had told her.

"*The Wizard of Oz* singalong is important. Either the Oz Killer timed the murder perfectly, or it's a coincidence."

"A big coincidence," Ona said.

"And then we have Sandy calling Dorothy a wicked witch. And we know what happens to the wicked witches in *The Wizard of Oz*."

"The Wicked Witch of the West melts when Dorothy throws water at her, right? But what about the Wicked Witch of the East…?"

Ona stopped herself.

Alice nodded, knowing her friend had remembered. "She gets crushed when Dorothy's house falls on her. It's not a batten—but still…"

Sandy Spiegel's home stood at the end of a dirt road

among pine trees, with a bubbling brook snaking around the property. Under different circumstances, it would've looked magical. But this morning, the sight of Chief Jimbo's cruiser marred the idyllic setting.

Ona parked the pickup and Alice jumped out.

Sandy, a blonde woman in her sixties, must've been 6 ft. 6 and as broad-shouldered as a giant. She stood on the porch talking to Chief Jimbo, who looked like a Munchkin next to her. He greeted Alice with a hesitant smile, a look of worry on his face.

"Is everything all right?" Alice asked.

"Not all right," Sandy snapped. She gestured behind her. "I spent last night at Lorraine's place, and when I got back here this morning, I find someone's broken into my home."

"You were telling me," Chief Jimbo said, holding his pen and notepad ready, "what's missing…"

"The dirty rat raided the pantry. Bread. Canned beans and fruit. Chips and salsa. He got into the fridge, too. Cheese. Ham. Mayo. All gone. A couple of bottles of wine. A fine bourbon I got as a gift. Other stuff, too. Toilet paper."

Chief Jimbo looked up from his note taking. "Toilet paper?"

"That's what I said, wasn't it? He also took an entire stack of old newspapers and magazines."

"He?"

"Well, obviously it was that wild man living in the woods."

"What makes you say that?"

"My brain," Sandy said, and Chief Jimbo blushed and looked down at his notes.

Then Sandy rounded on Alice and Ona. "What are you two doing here?"

"I'm so sorry to hear about the break-in…" Alice began.

"Come on. Spit it out. No dilly-dally."

Alice and Ona exchanged a glance. "Well," Alice said,

seeing no other option but to tell the truth, "we heard you had a meeting with Dorothy about *The Wizard of Oz* singalong."

"My Lord," Sandy said, throwing up her giant hands. "Can't a woman disagree with another woman without being accused of murder?"

"I wasn't accusing you—"

"Oh, I know very well what you were getting at." Sandy narrowed her eyes. "I bet that little rat, Mr. Gorny, told you. Nasty little man."

"He simply said—"

"That I called Dorothy a wicked witch? Well, so what? She was a wicked witch. And a lousy, two-faced liar. She agreed to an *Oz* singalong, and then, at the last minute, canceled. And for what? To put on *Grease*." She let out a huff to show her disdain. "A movie named after the filth from a garage tells you a lot about its quality. Garbage. Dorothy was putting on garbage and calling it culture. But I gave her a piece of my mind…"

"Can you tell us more about the singalong?"

"No." Sandy glared at Chief Jimbo. "And you—why are you standing around like a lump? Go take a look at the scene of the crime. Get to work!"

"Yes, ma'am," Chief Jimbo mumbled, and headed inside the house.

Sandy followed him. She turned and aimed her glare at Ona, then Alice.

"And you two. Get off my property."

She slammed the door.

CHAPTER 17

*T*hat night, the three friends—Alice, Becca, and Ona
—met at the Woodlander Bar.

To Alice, the Woodlander Bar, a tiny house nestled in the
woods, epitomized Blithedale's coziness. Hurricane lanterns
glowed at the edges of the pebble-strewn area where the
tables sat, while lanterns dangled overheard. Music drifted
across the space—mellifluous classical guitar tracks mixed
with mellow bluegrass instrumentals.

"I love this place," Becca said.

Getting a night off was a rare occurrence for her, and she
was clearly savoring every moment. Alice was enjoying it,
too. Her mind kept circling the encounter with Sandy, and
yet she avoided the topic in front of Becca and Ona.

Tonight's about having fun, she told herself. *We won't talk
murder.*

They sat at a table near the tiny house bar, which Ona had
built for the owner, Thor.

Thor emerged from the tiny house with their drinks on a
tray, his long blonde hair swaying in the evening breeze. The
Woodlander Bar wasn't busy yet—and when he could, he

liked to come out from behind the bar and talk to customers. Alice enjoyed his company, not the least because he was easy on the eyes: If he hadn't become a bartender, he could have been a model.

"This is my new apple cider martini."

Alice sipped her cocktail.

"It's delicious, Thor. Is that a hint of cinnamon? When I make a cocktail, it involves pouring tonic water and gin into a glass with ice and hoping for the best. I don't know how you do it."

"I take my time," Thor said. "There's this Danish philosopher, Kierkegaard, he said we're so busy chasing pleasure that we hurry past it. I think he's right. Slow down when you make a cocktail. Slow down when you drink it. Consider each sip and see how it feels."

After he left, she took his advice. She took a sip, closing her eyes to be sure she really tasted it and felt it. Now she tasted more than the apple and cinnamon. The sharpness of lemon juice and alcohol mellowed by maple syrup. Memories of apple pie coming straight out of the oven…hot cider warming her hands on a cold day…sugary apple cider donuts…

She opened her eyes. Becca was grinning.

"What?"

Alice turned to Ona, who was also smiling.

"Come on," Alice said. "What's so funny?"

Becca said, "He's got you under his spell."

"This drink has me under its spell." She took another sip. "Yup, I'm in love with this drink. I think I'll marry it."

"And not Thor?"

Alice smiled. "A woman could do worse. But honestly, I've had enough of the marrying game. I've got my prize right here, thank you very much."

She raised her glass in a toast.

"To friends," she said.

Ona and Becca raised their glasses. "To friends!"

They drank.

Then, to Alice's disappointment, talk turned to the murder investigation. Ona told Becca about their encounter with Sandy.

Becca laughed. "Oh, Sandy Spiegel's always been a grouch. When it comes to emotions, she's like a bull. She sees red and—pow!—she's leveled the whole china shop."

"Dorothy was a bull, too."

"Right. So, you put two testy bulls in a china shop, and what do you think happens?"

Alice had tried to stay out of the conversation, but Becca's dismissiveness bothered her.

"You don't think Sandy's behavior is suspicious?" Alice asked.

"Suspicious?" Becca shook her head. "It would be suspicious if she acted all sweet."

"But she threatened Dorothy," Alice said. "And the killer was sending some kind of *Wizard of Oz*-related message."

Becca raised an eyebrow. "Are you seriously suggesting that Sandy murdered Dorothy Bowers because she canceled her *Oz* singalong?"

Alice frowned. She took another sip of her drink, trying to hide what she felt. Frustration. But also embarrassment—a sense of shame that she didn't understand. The truth that once Becca put the idea into plain words, Alice could see how ridiculous it seemed. But what if there was more to the encounter between Dorothy and Sandy? What if their disagreement went deeper? Sandy had slammed the door in their faces—if she had nothing to hide, why turn them away like that?

She kept her doubts to herself for now. Becca seemed so certain that Sandy was innocent. She knew everyone in town, which gave her a big advantage. But couldn't it also be a weakness, making her fail to suspect an old neighbor and friend, even if the person behaved suspiciously?

Maybe my strength is that I stand apart from everyone else—I can see things with an outsider's perspective.

Mayor MacDonald approached their table, interrupting her thoughts. He was wearing his usual white Mark Twain suit and twirled a cane as he came toward them.

"A friendly reminder, ladies. Tomorrow night, the Pointed Firs will play live here at the Woodlander Bar. Make sure you come." He spread out his arms, lifting his cane to the sky. "We're telling the whole world."

Beyond him, Alice could see others—Andrea from Bonsai & Pie and Esther from Love Again among them—moving from table to table, apparently also drumming up support for the Pointed Firs concert.

"No need to strong arm us," Ona said with a grin. "I love bluegrass. I'll come to any show of theirs."

"We'll be there," Alice said, trying to sound cheerful.

She'd just had a less-than-cheerful thought. Would the movie theater be opening again this weekend? Beau might face an empty auditorium. Because in a competition between old movies and bluegrass music, she didn't think the Blithedale Theater stood a chance.

CHAPTER 18

Saturday morning found Alice and Ona drinking coffee on the front steps of Wonderland Books when a troop of young people marched toward the store.

Even at a distance, the leader of the pack's black hair was unmistakable.

"Billy Brine," Alice said. "Now, what does he want? And who are all those people following him?"

"If they had pitchforks, they could play extras in Frankenstein," Ona said, sipping her coffee. "Though I'm guessing they're something much more mundane: podcast fans."

Alice got to her feet, as did Ona, getting out of the way. Billy Brine and his followers descended on the store like a swarm of locusts, pressing inside the tiny house. Within minutes, they'd pulled dozens of books from shelves, leaving them on the little benches, the counter, or resting face-down in sections where they didn't belong. Alice, having retreated to safety behind the counter, tried not to feel annoyed.

It's part of the business, she told herself. *I'm grateful to have customers.*

Ona was by her side, and now leaned close. "It's almost

impossible to tell how upset you are, except for the fact that you're grinding your teeth." But her tone was sympathetic, and she added, with a visible shudder, "Can you imagine the damage they'd do to the Pemberley Inn?"

Alice had an apocalyptic vision of the Pemberley Inn laid to waste, portraits hanging askew, wallpaper ripped, windows broken. Then her mind pictured Main Street thronged with savage podcast fans, roaming the streets like zombies.

She shuddered.

"Speaking of which, why aren't you at the inn, in case they want to book a room?"

Ona laughed. "These kids? Book accommodation at my hoity-toity inn? Forget about it. They're staying at a barn somewhere. Something Billy arranged for a song and a dance. I'll bet you 20 bucks they don't buy any books."

"Morning," Chief Jimbo said, coming into the store.

"What brings you to my bookshop?" Alice asked.

She got her answer when Billy hailed Chief Jimbo from across the store. "Chief, you ready?"

"Ready when you are, Billy." Chief Jimbo turned to Alice and Ona with a grin. "Did you listen to Billy's new podcast episode? It dropped last night."

Dropped? Alice had the feeling Chief Jimbo was emulating language that wasn't in his natural vocabulary.

"No, I haven't had the pleasure of listening to it yet."

"Well, you should. Billy lays out his theory about the Oz Killer, and even points to where he's located."

"Oh?"

"Right here in the Blithedale Woods."

Alice thought of the wild man she'd seen. The man who'd broken into Sandy's home, the public library, and—almost—Dorothy's place. She sighed. If Ona hadn't shown up early this morning, she might've had a chance to sneak away and take another look at Sandy's place. She couldn't get into Dorothy's home, of course, not now that Beau had put in a security system. And who knew where the wild man was hiding.

Well, apparently Billy does...

"After releasing the new episode," Chief Jimbo continued, "he put out a call to his followers—"

Billy himself came over and cut in. "And they jumped in cars and on buses, and here they are. Ready to hunt the killer."

Alice looked at Billy, then over at Chief Jimbo.

"Hunt the Oz Killer?"

Chief Jimbo nodded eagerly. If he'd had a tail, he would've wagged it. "Yeah, Billy's helping me do a manhunt. He found footprints behind the theater. They run along the river, heading south. So that's where we're going. We're going to catch the guy that killed Dorothy."

Billy smiled. "By tonight, we'll have bagged the bastard—and I'll be famous. Come on, Jimbo. Let's go."

He turned and called to his followers.

"Everyone. Meet up by Old Mayor Townsend's statue. We're leaving in 5 minutes."

As soon as Billy stepped outside with Chief Jimbo, most of his followers—short-haired, long-haired, pimpled, fake-tanned, they ran the whole gamut of youth—rushed for the door, clearly committed to sticking close to their fearless leader.

A couple of them came to the counter—both purple-haired girls. One had found a used paperback of Truman Capote's *In Cold Blood* for $3.99. The other put down a battered paperback on the counter—a $1.99 copy of Theodore Dreiser's *An American Tragedy*.

"Have you read these?" the girl who was buying *In Cold Blood* asked.

"Capote, yes," Alice said, ringing up the sale. "Dreiser, no."

"We're going to read both," the other said with a grin and a glance at her companion. "Then trade notes."

They kept stealing glances at each other, and the frustration Alice had felt melted away, replaced with the warmth of witnessing young love. She thought of Mr. and Mrs. Oriel, who had been giving each other those looks for decades, and wondered if these two, forty or fifty years down the line, would be cozied up in bed with a Brother Cadfael mystery, too.

She smiled. "That sounds like a great way to spend time together. Nothing better than a book."

"You should read Jane Austen," Ona said. "Just saying."

"Ona's always promoting Austen. As if she needed any PR."

One of the girls nodded. "Oh, she's amazing. We've read all of Austen—and the Brontë sisters, too."

"We haven't worked up our courage to read all of George Elliot's books yet," the other added.

"We will, though."

"Oh, yeah. Definitely. *Middlemarch* was mind blowing."

Alice liked the two young women so much that for a moment she'd forgotten that they hadn't simply come to Blithedale to buy books at Wonderland. They might be nice, but weren't they the first signs of the dark times to come? She thought of the killer dentist, and how hordes of journalists and horror fans had ruined that little town.

"What made you join Billy Brine's entourage?"

One girl shrugged. "He's making history. Or at least trying to."

"Billy comes across as confident," the other said. "But it's not easy to be successful in podcasting. He might be trending now. But next week he'll be back to working as a barista to pay the rent."

"Oh, he'll be fine," her friend said. "I hear he's got family with money to fall back on. Like a trust fund, or something."

"Actually, I heard it was just a job. A cousin or uncle or someone like that was offering a job. But it's not like it's what he wants to do."

"Which is to solve the great unsolved cases."

"Yeah, like *all* of them."

They seemed so earnest that Alice didn't have the heart to tell them that no one—let alone the FBI—would solve *all* the unsolved cases. And what about the "great ones" abroad? Did Billy Brine have the smarts to finally solve the Jack the Ripper case? She doubted it.

She handed them their change and their books, and they thanked her.

"We'd better hurry."

"Yeah, everyone's leaving soon."

"Bye!"

Alice watched them bound across the street, heading toward the Pemberley Inn and the statue of Old Mayor Townsend. She couldn't convince herself that these delightful girls were dangerous. Instead of feeling worried about their effect on Blithedale, she felt worried for their safety.

"I hope they'll be careful. What if they actually stumble on the Oz Killer?"

Ona chuckled. "Fat chance."

Alice eyed her friend. Ona gave her an amused smirk, and her one visible eye twinkled almost as much as the rhinestones on her eye patch.

"What do you know that I don't?"

"They're heading south to hunt the killer."

"So?"

"Well, which side of Main Street is the public library on?

Where does Sandy live? Where is Dorothy's house located? And what about Beau's cabin?"

Alice thought for a moment. Then realized what Ona was saying, and a burden lifted off her shoulders. "North. The wild man has only been spotted on the north side and Billy Brine is going south." Relieved, she laughed. "They're looking in the wrong place."

CHAPTER 19

*A*fter Billy Brine and his entourage left, Wonderland Books subsided to the usual Saturday rhythm of customers coming and going. Ona returned to the inn. Watching her friend go, Alice had to admit that Ona's insight about Billy's misguided manhunt wasn't one she would've made. If Ona hadn't been around, she would've closed the bookshop and chased Billy and his followers.

Gone on a wild goose chase.

Maybe Becca and Ona were right. Maybe she didn't know what she was doing. Maybe she should stick to her books.

The truth was that she relished her work—chatting with people about their lives and their reading habits, finding just the right book to make them happy, broadening their horizons with a new author they might never have considered.

Blithedale was a small town, and despite the Blithedale Future Fund's aspirations, it wasn't a shopping destination yet. However, the area remained a favorite weekend destination for hikers, leaf peepers, and other nature lovers, and today, as on other days, Alice sold multiple copies of *Walden*, *Wild*, and *A Walk in the Woods*.

A group of 30-something friends, looking so pristine in their new hiking gear they could've stepped out of an REI catalog, browsed the shelves and talked and laughed, and one of them soon drew Alice into a conversation about his love of Victorian literature.

"They don't write books like that anymore. I mean, is there anything more exciting and atmospheric than Wilkie Collins or Charles Dickens or Emily Brontë?"

Alice agreed that Brontë, Collins, and Dickens were incredible.

"And when it comes to the detective story, what's better than Sherlock Holmes?" the guy continued. "Whenever I read contemporary fiction, I'm disappointed. It's so—" He sighed. "—recognizable."

Alice laughed. "That sounds like a challenge, and I can't resist a challenge."

She led him to the shelves and pulled out a paperback and handed it to him.

He studied the cover.

"Philip Pullman. *The Ruby in the Smoke*." He looked up. "Wait, doesn't Pullman write fantasy or science fiction? I'm not not into fantasy and sci-fi."

"You're thinking of the *His Dark Materials* series. That's fantasy sci-fi—and also brilliant—but if you want an atmospheric Victorian yarn with lots of penny dreadful thrills and memorable characters, you can't go wrong with the Sally Lockhart mysteries."

He opened the book to page one. She watched him read the first paragraph of the first chapter. His eyes widened. He looked up. "Oh, this is good."

She rang up the purchases—the others had found their fair share of fiction and nonfiction books. As they left Wonderland, their happy chatter drifting down Main Street with them, the tiny house grew surprisingly still.

But one customer remained in a corner, a customer she hadn't noticed come in. He'd found a bench and sat cross-legged, his rumpled gray suit riding up his ankles and exposing his garish Winnie-the-Pooh socks.

Leonard Stout, the county coroner.

Alice greeted him. "Morning, Lenny. What brings you to Wonderland Books on this beautiful day?"

"Good morning," he said morosely. "If it is a good morning, which I doubt. Anyway, it's not one I can spend browsing books for long, however much I'd like to." He let out a long, heavy sigh. "There's no rest for the weary. The work never stops."

"More crimes?"

"More dead people. Every day, they die. Almost as much as they're born." He glanced at the book he'd been flipping through. It was a collection of poems by Seamus Heaney. "I've read this one before. His poem about the Tollund Man, a mummified corpse from the Iron Age, is unforgettable. Guess I'll read it again."

Somehow the idea of the county coroner reading poems about corpses in his spare time made Alice feel sad. Surely, he wanted to forget about death when he picked up a book. Unless it was a cozy mystery or a Golden Age detective novel.

"Are you looking for a new author? A new book?"

He shuddered. "Good grief, no. Why would I subject myself to that kind of torture? I read what I've read before until I've got it firmly under my skin."

"But you must read something new—or else how can you ever have anything to reread?"

He looked up at her, pursing his lips as he considered her question. "That's a puzzle I've often tried to solve. In the meantime, I'll stick with my favorites. I collect them. I reread them. They're like good old friends who take my mind off the work. Especially cases like the Dorothy Bowers death."

He shook his head, his sad eyes seeming to droop even further.

"The Oz Killer," she said.

He gave her a sharp look. "So everyone says."

"You don't believe it?"

He shrugged. "I'm not at liberty to discuss the case."

"I understand," Alice said.

In that instant, an idea flashed across her mind. If she'd thought too long and hard on it, she might have talked herself out of it, hesitating to do a thing that could only be dubbed *dubious*. Morally. Legally. Definitely dubious.

But in the seconds that it took her to skip back behind the counter and dig out the first edition of *The House at Pooh Corner*, she thought only of pleasing Lenny Stout—and what pleasing him might do.

He received the book with almost religious reverence, and he ran a hand across the cover before turning it over to study the back. He gently turned the pages. He even lifted the open book to his face and inhaled the smell.

"Aah," he said. Then said, "Are you sure you're willing to part with this?"

"If it finds the right home, I'm happy." She smiled and added, "Besides, it's a little worn and its dust jacket is ripped. As a first edition, it won't be worth much more than its original list price. But you can have it."

He looked at her, one eyebrow raised.

"As a gift," she added.

"And you don't expect anything in return? No strings attached?"

She bit her lip, wishing she could bargain for details from the case. But she shook her head. "No strings."

He clutched the book to his chest like a teddy bear. His

droopy eyes were no less sad, and yet the way he held the book told Alice that she'd brought him real joy.

He turned to go. But halfway through the doorway, he stopped. His back was still turned to her. He sighed, his shoulders moving up and down. He said, "There's always strings attached."

Speaking in a quiet voice, and still hugging the book to his chest, he said, "When the so-called Oz Killer murdered Dorothy Smith, the press made much of the connection with *The Wizard of Oz.* They pointed to how the presumed killer, Arthur Crumpit, had been obsessed with the L. Frank Baum books. The assumption was that Crumpit drew inspiration from the book, and left a twisted tribute to Oz at the scene of the crime."

"The ruby-red sneakers."

Lenny held up a finger. "The press, if I remember correctly, simply said 'sparkling shoes like the ones little Dorothy wore in *The Wizard of Oz.*' We never released the full details, aware that there might be copycats."

A memory niggled the back of Alice's mind. A detail she'd overlooked. But what?

"The ruby-red sneakers—there was something about them you didn't tell the public?"

Lenny nodded. "In the old film with Judy Garland, Dorothy wears ruby-red slippers. That was a deliberate choice to take advantage of the new Technicolor technology."

Alice put a hand to her mouth, the insight jolting her.

"But in L. Frank Baum's book, Dorothy doesn't wear ruby-red slippers."

Lenny nodded.

"Silver shoes," she said. "In the book, Dorothy wears silver shoes."

"And so did Dorothy Smith when she died. She was found wearing silver shoes."

CHAPTER 20

"*T*here is no Oz Killer," Alice said, to the astonishment of both Becca and Ona. She'd called them both and insisted they meet at the diner, then put up her "Sorry, We're Closed" sign and rushed off. Now the three of them sat in a booth, huddled together, keeping their voices low.

Becca sipped her coffee and looked thoughtful. Ona furrowed her brows, only one showing since the other was hidden by her rhinestone eye patch.

"Wait, wait," Ona said. "Let me see if I've got this right. Dorothy Smith was killed by Arthur Crumpit. But the police never caught him."

Alice nodded. "Lenny Stout said all the evidence pointed to him, and he, Lenny, believes Crumpit killed himself. But until they can find more evidence, it's technically an unsolved case."

"Then Dorothy Johnson," Ona said, "was poisoned by her dentist. He used the media frenzy around the Oz Killer to divert attention from what he was doing, putting her in ruby-red shoes to make it look like Crumpit did it."

"Right. But what the dentist didn't know was that Arthur Crumpit was obsessed with the books, not the movie. He put Dorothy Smith in silver shoes, not ruby-red ones. Whoever killed Dorothy Bowers made the same mistake."

Becca slapped a hand on the table, and the coffee cups jumped. "That bastard."

"Crumpit?"

"No. Whoever the killer is. He, she, *they* wanted to make us think this was about someone outside of Blithedale. Some crazy guy who targeted Dorothy Bowers because of her name. But in fact, the killer is one of us. Someone who knew poor Dorothy and had a personal reason for killing her."

She glared at her coffee cup, lapsing into thought again.

Alice watched her friends digest the new information. She felt good about sharing this breakthrough with them. Now they would see what she was capable of—she just needed some space to do things her way.

Alice said, "The question then is why did the killer use the Oz Killer? Why not some other serial killer?"

"*The Wizard of Oz* singalong," Ona suggested.

"That means either the killer picked it, because it was convenient or—"

"—or the murder is related to the singalong."

Alice and Ona nodded, considering this conclusion.

"Ruby red sneakers," Becca said thoughtfully. "I knew I'd seen ruby-red sneakers in Blithedale before…"

"Where?!" Alice and Ona said in unison.

"On a shelf at Love Again," Becca said. "Esther's consignment store."

Alice shot to her feet, eager to get to the consignment store. Ona put a hand on her arm. Gently, she said, "I'm coming with you."

CHAPTER 21

*E*sther Lucas held up the glittery red sneakers.

"This is the last pair. I tell you, I'm glad I didn't order more. Sandy Spiegel told me hundreds of people would be going to the singalong—and just as many would be lining up to buy these sneakers. But only one person did."

Alice and Ona, having rushed down Main Street, stood in the bright, airy consignment store with its racks of colorful clothes, and Alice could hardly contain her excitement. Finally, a breakthrough.

"Who bought the sneakers?"

"Why, Sandy herself, of course."

Alice and Ona exchanged a look. Sandy Spiegel, who had called Dorothy a witch. Sandy Spiegel, who had slammed the door in their faces when they'd asked her questions.

Esther put the sneakers back on the shelf. "In fact, she bought two pairs."

"Two?"

"One for herself and one for Lorraine."

"Lorraine, the librarian?" Alice asked.

Esther nodded. "They're best friends."

Alice thought of Lorraine, the friendly librarian, and refused to believe that she could be a killer. But Sandy Spiegel...

"I told Chief Jimbo all this," Esther added. "I also told him there's no way Sandy could be the Oz Killer..."

"Well, if the shoe fits..."

"That's the thing," Esther said. "The shoe wouldn't fit. The shoes she bought for herself—they would be way too big for Dorothy's feet. Sandy wears a size 14. I had to order the ruby-red shoes from a special supplier."

"What about the other pair? Would they have fit Dorothy's feet?"

Esther fretfully twirled a strand of black hair on her finger. "Well..."

"They're the same size, aren't they?"

She nodded. "Dorothy wore a size 9 shoe. So does Lorraine."

CHAPTER 22

*B*y the time Alice and Ona got there, the public library was closed for the day. A plywood board covered the broken door, and a sign pointed to a side entrance, where another told them it was "closed." So they jumped into Ona's pickup truck and drove north—into the Blithedale Woods.

As the pickup bumped down the rutted dirt road and Sandy's home came into sight among the trees, Alice spotted a car parked by the porch.

"Whose car is that?"

"Look at the bumper stickers," Ona said.

Stickers covering the back of the old, dirt-splattered Honda included "Support Your Public Library"; "Don't Make Me Use My Librarian Voice"; and "The Book Is Always Better Than the Movie."

"Lorraine is here," Alice said.

Ona turned the pickup, pulling up next to the Honda, and the truck came to a shuddering halt. The two of them got out. They had hardly slammed the doors before Sandy ducked out of her doorway. She wore a red-and-black flannel shirt and stood with her arms crossed, scowling, looking as big as Paul Bunyan.

"What do you two want?"

Behind her, Lorraine appeared, and when she saw Alice and Ona she smiled and waved.

"Hi!"

Sandy turned to Lorraine. "You know these two?"

"Of course I do. Well, everyone knows Ona from the Pemberley Inn, and Alice runs the new bookstore."

"I get my books at the public library," Sandy said, and threw Alice an accusatory glance.

"That's all right, Sandy," Lorraine said, putting a hand on her friend's arm. "Bookstores and public libraries are friends. We're not competing. Besides, libraries aren't just about books—we're about offering a public space. Where else can people go without having to buy anything? Where else can anyone—regardless of who they are or how they're dressed— go and spend the entire day? And not to forget, get information. Just the other day, Alice and Ona dropped by to get help with some research."

"Research?" Sandy said suspiciously. "What kind of research?"

"About the Oz Killer."

"Good grief. If one more person asks me about that…"

Alice swallowed. Sandy looked like she could split wood with her bare hands.

Lorraine squeezed her friend's arm and leaned close. "Calm down, Sandy. They mean no harm. They want to help, is all."

Sandy snorted, as if she found that hard to believe. But then she said, "Fine. You've come all the way out here for a reason. What is it?"

Alice and Ona exchanged a look.

"Ruby red sneakers," Alice said. "You bought a pair from Esther Lucas."

"I bought two pairs. One for me. One for Lorraine." Sandy's face darkened. "We were going to wear them for *The Wizard of Oz* singalong before that woman canceled it."

"She means poor Dorothy," Lorraine added, a mournful look on her face. "What a horrible tragedy."

"I already told Chief Jimbo all about it," Sandy said.

"Oh," Alice said. "So he took them away as evidence."

Sandy laughed. Her booming laughter was so deep and loud it sent birds fluttering away from their branches.

"Don't be ridiculous. Chief Jimbo took my word for it and hurried back to town."

Why didn't that surprise Alice? Chief Jimbo wasn't exactly known for his thoroughness.

"Can we see the shoes?" Ona asked. She grinned and pointed at her eye patch. "You know how I love glittery things."

"Fine."

Sandy turned around and tromped into the house, ducking to avoid bumping her head on the lintel.

"Do you still have yours?" Ona asked.

Left alone with Alice and Ona, Lorraine suddenly took an interest in the trees. She rubbed the back of her neck. She shifted from foot to foot.

"Yes, what about your shoes, Lorraine?" Alice asked.

"Oh, they're somewhere. You know," Lorraine said and forced a smile, "we had planned that singalong months and months ago, or Sandy had. It was her idea. She convinced Dorothy to put it on. It was such a disappointment when it was canceled."

"We heard Sandy had a meeting with Dorothy."

Lorraine nodded. "She lost her temper. She often does. But I convinced her we could still celebrate Oz on our own."

"How?"

"Saturday night, we stayed here at Sandy's and had a *Wizard of Oz*-themed dinner, with heart-shaped burgers for the Lion, mashed potato brains for the Tin Woodman, and cake with green melted witch's icing on top. We ate dinner while watching the movie."

Ona smiled. "An all-nighter Oz fest?"

"Oh, we're both early birds. So we watched the movie and then went to bed. I slept on the couch."

"So I guess you were at Sandy's all of Saturday night?"

Lorraine looked away. "As I said, I went to bed early on the couch. Then we had a big breakfast in the morning and listened to *The Wizard of Oz* soundtrack on Sandy's stereo."

There was a crash from inside the house. Then another crash, and Lorraine's eyes widened.

"My goodness…"

The three of them rushed inside. The rustic house was well furnished with wood furniture. Even the couch was made of wood, with cushions placed on top.

Inside a bedroom at the back, Sandy was throwing items out of a closet. Shoe boxes. Tennis rackets. A crate full of old CDs.

"Where are they? I've looked in the shoe rack. I've looked in the hallway closet. This is the last place they could be. Unless—"

She swung around and dropped to all fours with a thump. Then pressed herself to the floor.

"This can't be… "

She reached a long arm underneath the bed and moved things around. Meanwhile, Alice glanced at the massive bed. A bedside table held a stack of library books, a water glass, and a vial of prescription sleeping pills.

Sandy let out an exasperated growl.

"I never misplace stuff."

She got to her feet, rising close to the ceiling. She scratched her head.

"My ruby-red sneakers," she said. "They're gone."

"Gone?" Alice said.

"That burglar—I bet he took them."

CHAPTER 23

*A*t the Woodlander Bar, Alice took a sip of Thor's Saturday night special. It was an Old Vermont gin cocktail with lemon and orange juice, Angostura bitters, and maple syrup.

"There's only one thing more suspicious than the theft of the shoes."

Ona nodded. "Lorraine's behavior."

"She was clearly lying—or at least not telling us the whole truth."

It felt good to talk to Ona. It felt good to be together. Showing Becca and Ona that she could reach a breakthrough in the case—the details she'd learned from Lenny Stout—had renewed her confidence. But she hadn't solved the case yet. And tonight she wouldn't make any progress.

They'd arrived early for the bluegrass concert, which turned out to be a good decision as almost every table was already taken, and more people were coming in every minute. People crowded the bar in the tiny house, and after a group of friends sat down at the last table outside, late-comers had to settle for standing.

Thor, the owner of the Woodlander Bar, had moved a few tables to make space for the Pointed Firs bluegrass trio. The three women got their instruments ready—a guitar, banjo, and washboard.

Then the audience fell into an almost absolute silence, waiting for the music to start.

Smiling, the three musicians looked at each other. The banjo player nodded her head. They launched into a spirited instrumental, with the washboard and guitar acting as rhythm instruments and the banjo picking the tune.

All around the Woodlander Bar, people grinned and stomped their feet. Alice herself found it impossible not to tap her foot, and she caught Ona grinning at her.

"I wish Becca could be here for this," she said.

"Me too."

Saturday night was a busy time at the diner, and Becca couldn't leave Susan to manage everything on her own. She didn't seem to mind, though, loving her business as she did. More than a source of BLTs and burgers, the diner was a sanctuary for people to find solace. There was a Dickens quote on the wall in the diner: "No one is useless in this world who lightens the burden of it to anyone else."

Alice said, "I understand why Becca's so devoted to her diner. I feel there wouldn't be a Blithedale without the What the Dickens Diner."

Ona nodded. "Ever since I moved here a few years ago, the diner's been like a home away from home."

"I feel the same way," Alice said, "and about the Pemberley Inn, too."

"The inn is your home, silly."

Alice said no more. She felt a twinge of the old guilt, her mind going to the many nights and days she'd lived for free at Ona's inn.

They focused their attention once more on the music. But

Alice continued to think about her situation. Soon, she'd need to move out of the Pemberley Inn. She glanced at Ona, who was bobbing her head to the music, and thought, *It'll be better when I'm not taking advantage of you anymore, Ona. You'll see.*

She remembered the first time she'd contributed to household finances at her aunt and uncle's. After her mom died, Alice had moved in with her aunt and uncle, a childless couple, and although they never said so, she'd always felt like she was a burden. So, as soon as she had the chance, she'd done chores for neighbors—walking dogs, mowing lawns, tidying homes—to earn money for groceries and her "rent." Her aunt and uncle had been surprised, she remembered that much. But they'd taken the money and praised her for her diligence. Obviously, it had made a difference.

Ever since then, Alice had worked to be self-reliant.

In a way, she reflected, that self-reliance had brought her to Blithedale. How else could she have been strong enough to walk away from the comforts of her life with Rich Crawford, her ex-fiancé?

The bluegrass band finished a song and the audience clapped and cheered.

As the band leaped into another number, Alice looked out across the audience and saw Mayor MacDonald in his white suit. Esther Lucas sat at a table with Andrea Connor, the owner of the Bonsai & Pie cafe. Chief Jimbo sat at another table talking to a couple of men in hunting vests. He was out of his uniform, wearing a flannel shirt and jeans instead, which made him blend in with the larger crowd.

As she watched, one of the men in vests slapped Jimbo on the back and the other laughed. Jimbo smiled uneasily and took a sip of beer, trying to hide his embarrassment at whatever the other man had said.

Alice felt a stab of sympathy for him. Here was a man

who wasn't comfortable in his own skin. A man whom everyone in town thought was a failure. He didn't know how to do his job, and half the time, he shirked his responsibilities. But he wasn't mean—and she suspected that, deep down, he wanted success and recognition.

She drew her attention away from Jimbo and watched the bluegrass trio. They finished another rousing tune, then subsided into a ballad sung by the banjo player, her voice so rich and warm, it melted the crowd. Alice felt herself mesmerized by the woman's singing.

Then their first set was over. The audience burst into applause again. People hollered and stomped, and the trio bowed. Thor emerged from the tiny house with a tray of drinks, which he brought straight to the musicians.

"You deserve a break and a drink," he said.

"Hear, hear," someone in the audience shouted.

Another round of applause erupted.

The banjo player, drink in hand, drifted through the crowd and came to Alice and Ona's table.

"How were we, Ona?"

"Incredible, as always," Ona said. "But I've got to admit, I think tonight was the best ever."

Alice said, "I agree. The whole set was amazing, but that last song…my knees went weak."

The woman smiled. "Thank you."

She introduced herself as Althea Strong.

"I remember you, of course," she told Alice. "We played at your bookstore's grand opening."

"I haven't forgotten—thanks to your music, you drew the whole town to my tiny bookshop. But I was so busy, we never got a chance to talk."

"Busy is good." She took a sip of her drink. "In fact, we've been getting more and more gigs, and we were hoping for a big one here in town, but then poor Dorothy died."

Alice frowned. "Sorry, I don't understand. How does Dorothy play a part?"

"She'd promised us a gig at the Blithedale Theater. A big concert with lots of promotion."

"But the Blithedale Theater only shows movies," Alice said. "The closest to live events are those singalongs."

Althea shrugged. "I got the feeling Dorothy was ready to change things. Shake 'em up. Speaking of which—" She looked at her wristwatch. "—it's time for me and the ladies to start our second set."

She drained her drink and headed back to her fellow musicians, leaving Alice to think about what she'd said. Could it be true that Dorothy had big changes planned? It would make sense. Why else had she wanted to get the support of the Blithedale Future Fund?

"I'll get us more drinks," Ona said.

But Alice grabbed the empty glasses before her friend could.

"Nope. My treat."

She headed toward the tiny house before Ona could protest. The least Alice could do was pay for drinks.

A crowd thronged the tiny bar, and as she inched closer, she watched Thor juggle shakers and glasses with a deftness that came close to magic.

Finally, when it was her turn, Thor grinned at her.

"Alice, what do you think of the concert?"

"I love it."

"I plan to do more—we don't have enough live music in Blithedale."

"Unless you count the *Grease* singalong," Alice said, joking.

Thor leaned forward and, shielding his mouth with his hand, said, "Don't tell anyone, but I went to the *Grease* singalong."

Alice laughed. "Your secret is safe with me."

"It was amazing. I got to wear my leather jacket and ripped jeans and sing along to 'Summer Nights.' What could be better? And I wasn't the only one dressed up. Andrea Connor was decked out as Betty Rizzo. And there was an entire group of guys, like me, dressed up as T-Birds. But the best outfit was Lorraine's. She was Frenchy, complete with a pink wig and—"

"Wait a minute," Alice said. "Did you say Lorraine?"

"Yeah, Lorraine. You know, the librarian."

"But she wasn't at the singalong. She was at Sandy's."

Thor shrugged. "Andrea, Lorraine, and I were the last to leave the theater. Unless Lorraine has a twin sister, I can guarantee it was her."

CHAPTER 24

*T*he next morning, the What the Dickens Diner was no less busy—in fact, Becca said it was busier than Saturday night.

"Seems half the town went to the Woodlander Bar last night, so after a mad dash at dinnertime, the diner calmed down early. But I guess people need a satisfying dinner before they do all that bluegrass foot-stomping—and a hearty breakfast the morning after."

Alice, who sat at the counter, looked around. The diner was packed, with every booth occupied. Becca smiled as she poured Alice another cup of coffee.

"You'll never hear me complain about a full house," she said.

"Any idea how it went at the theater last night?"

"Oh, the theater didn't open yet. Beau's taking his time. Between you and me, I think Mr. Gorny wanted to open, but Beau got cold feet. The poor guy's overwhelmed."

Becca moved off to serve other customers, leaving Alice with worried thoughts about how Beau would manage the theater. Susan, the waitress, whizzed past, a tray heaped with plates full of pancakes, eggs, and bacon. Alice raised her cup to sip her coffee and got as far as her lips and stopped. Because across the diner, she'd spotted someone she knew.

Lorraine was sitting alone in a booth, studying the menu. She glanced over her shoulder toward the door, apparently waiting for someone to arrive.

Alice put down her cup of coffee, and risking the loss of her seat at the counter, hurried across the diner.

"Morning, Lorraine."

Lorraine looked up, startled. Then recovered and smiled.

"Oh, hi, Alice. The diner's packed, isn't it? Sandy's joining me for breakfast. If you want to join us, you're welcome to."

"I won't bother you," Alice said. She cut to the chase. "I just have a question about the night Dorothy died. I spoke with Thor at the Woodlander Bar. He said he saw you at the theater."

Lorraine cast a nervous glance over her shoulder. "Um…"

Finally, she motioned for Alice to sit down.

"All right," she whispered, leaning across the table to speak with Alice in confidence. "I admit it. I was there. I didn't want to tell you and Ona, though, because I was worried Sandy would overhear."

"So you didn't stay the night at her place."

Lorraine sighed. "It's exactly as I told you: We had dinner, we watched *The Wizard of Oz*, we went to bed. After I bedded down on the couch, I waited for Sandy to fall asleep. She sleeps deeply."

Alice remembered something she'd seen at Sandy's. "She takes sleeping pills, doesn't she?"

Lorraine nodded. "Once she's fast asleep, moose stampeding through the house won't wake her. So that night, I got up, put on my sneakers—the red ones she'd bought me—and I got in my car and drove down to the theater, just in time to change into my *Grease* costume and join the festivities."

"But why all the sneaking around?"

"Sandy doesn't like *Grease*. And after Dorothy canceled *The Wizard of Oz* singalong and added *Grease* instead, she half blames the movie. I don't have the heart to tell her I love the musical."

"When Ona and I first came to see you at the library, you were listening to the soundtrack."

She nodded. "And the singalong was wonderful. I had a blast. I only wished Sandy could share my love of the musical. Then we could've gone together."

"Did you stay late?"

"I was one of the last to leave. Dorothy ushered us out at around 11 pm—me, Andrea, and Thor. It wasn't until I sneaked back into Sandy's place that I realized I was wearing the wrong shoes. I'd kept my Pink Lady shoes on. The next morning, I had to cover up—and hope Sandy didn't ask about the sneakers she got me. Luckily, she didn't notice."

"But the ruby-red sneakers…"

"I must've left them in the restroom at the theater."

"And the killer found them."

Lorraine grimaced. "I know. Somehow I feel responsible. If I hadn't left them behind…"

Alice believed her. In some ways, the guilt Lorraine showed was the most convincing thing. Alice put a hand on her arm. "This is huge."

"It is?"

"It means the killer didn't plan to stage Dorothy's murder in a way that connected it to the Oz Killer. Like the dentist who killed Dorothy Johnson, this murderer saw an opportunity to throw the police off the scent, and they took it."

Lorraine turned, looking toward the diner entrance, and Alice followed her gaze. Lorraine smiled. Sandy ducked through the doorway and came striding across the diner, drawing not a few glances for her striking height. The happiness that showed on Lorraine's face warmed Alice—the librarian clearly loved her friend and had only wanted to protect their friendship from any unhappiness.

Neither was a killer. Removing Lorraine and Sandy from the list of suspects was a relief.

Sandy had nearly reached the table when a ruckus made her stop and turn. The diner door had flung open and a group of young people came pouring in, led by their pied piper, Billy Brine.

"We know where the Oz Killer is," he announced. "He's hiding north of town. After pancakes, we're gonna get him. And thanks to my podcast, the whole world will be paying attention."

CHAPTER 25

"It doesn't seem very wise," Alice said, back at the diner counter. It was a huge understatement. As far as she could tell, this was a potential disaster. Billy had worked out that the wild man must be north of town. By broadcasting the manhunt, he would attract more outsiders with a morbid interest in Dorothy's murder. And—she thought of the purple-haired girls—risk the lives of a bunch of impressionable kids.

"There's a wisdom of the head and there's a wisdom of the heart," Becca said, apparently paraphrasing Dickens, "and I doubt young Billy has either."

"Oh, he's not a bad kid," Mr. Gorny said, as he slipped onto the stool next to Alice's. He asked for coffee while he looked at the menu.

It surprised Alice that the conservative Mr. Gorny, defender of the Bowers tradition, would be so positive about Billy Brine. Her surprise must've shown, because he added, "Sure, I used to turn my nose up at these newfangled podcasts. But Billy's set me straight. It's just a radio show, isn't it? What's so new about that? Anyway, you've got to admire the kid—he's got pluck."

He glanced back at Billy, who had somehow commandeered a booth, his followers piling in—and those who didn't get a seat stood crowded around it. Billy himself remained standing, lecturing his crew on how to catch a killer. Their chatter spiked the volume in the diner, and several locals glanced over, frowns of irritation on their faces.

Mr. Gorny turned back to Becca, a frown gathering on his own face.

"A bran muffin, please. I don't have time for a full breakfast. I've got to give these kids a ride into the woods."

"You're chauffeuring them?" Becca asked as she poured coffee into a cup and slid it across the counter to Mr. Gorny. Mr. Gorny took a sip. Becca served him a bran muffin.

"They're staying at my place for a few bucks a head," he said. Then added with a shrug, "It's far from town, so the least I could do is give them a ride."

"They're all staying with you?" Alice asked, surprised.

"Camping in my barn."

"More like glamping," came a voice behind them, and Alice turned to see Billy sauntering toward them. "Mr. Gorny got everyone these great army cots—pretty good planning."

"Billy," Mr. Gorny snapped. He glanced at his watch, clearly impatient. "We're leaving soon. Are you going to eat breakfast or waste time talking?"

"Why'd you think I came up here? To speed things up a little. It's nice that the diner embraces the slow food movement, but what does it take to get breakfast served quickly? Bacon, pancakes, and eggs for me and my crew."

Becca frowned. "We embrace the right-on-time food movement, and more than anything, the be-kind-to-your-neighbor philosophy. Not to mention good manners."

"Oh, sorry." Billy exaggerated his words. He put on a fake smile. "Pretty please, can I have some breakfast?"

Alice wanted to slap Billy's smirk off his face. He seemed impervious to Becca's firm voice. But when Mr. Gorny barked his name—"Billy!"—the kid straightened up, showing signs of paying attention.

"You'll show some decency while you're in this town," Mr. Gorny said. "We don't tolerate hoodlums here—no matter who you are."

Billy's smile faded. "We'll eat breakfast quick," he muttered. "Then you can drive us north of town for our manhunt."

He turned away and heading back to the booth, his head held high.

"Kids," Mr. Gorny said. "Give 'em an inch…"

"What if Billy's wrong?" Alice asked, trying to cast doubt on the whole operation. "What if the wild man isn't hiding north of town? I mean, it's all speculation, right?"

Mr. Gorny shook his head. "That's clearly where the Oz Killer is hiding. And that's where Billy and his friends will be looking."

Alice bit her lip and looked over toward Billy.

The Oz Killer might be a fabrication, but she'd seen the wild man herself. He was living in the woods north of town, and he might be a real danger.

"There you are, Mr. Gorny."

Beau Bowers approached them at the counter, interrupting Alice's troubled thoughts. "I got your message to stop by before heading to Dorothy's place."

"Good. I'll help you clear out her things."

"There's no need. I can throw out old papers by myself."

Alice cut in. "Wait, you're just going to throw out Dorothy's papers?"

Beau rubbed his neck. "There's too much. I've been going

through everything, folder by folder, sheet by sheet, and at this rate, I'll be done with the job 20 years from now."

"Beau needs to focus on the theater," Mr. Gorny said. "You can't leave a business unopened for so long."

Alice agreed. But she thought of Dorothy's presentation for the Future Fund.

"I'm happy to help," she said.

Mr. Gorny held up a hand. "I agree with Alice. This is not a one-person job, Beau. You didn't remove any of her stuff yet, did you?"

"Not a thing."

Mr. Gorny said to Alice, "It's kind of you to offer. But this is theater business. Beau and I will handle it together. Once I take these kids to the woods, I'll come back to town and pick you up, Beau. We'll have plenty of time to clear out Dorothy's place before I need to drive the kids to the bus stop tonight."

Alice said, "So Billy and his friends are leaving Blithedale?"

"These kids have to catch the last bus," Mr. Gorny said. "They're going back to school and work tomorrow."

"Billy, too?"

Mr. Gorny shrugged. "Billy might stay for a few more days." He drained his coffee. "Enough dawdling. Let's get this show on the road."

He headed toward Billy and his entourage. Alice and Beau watched Mr. Gorny shepherd the group of young people out of the diner with the firmness of a school teacher—or rather, a movie theater usher. He could be brusque, but the fact that he was willing to host this pack of young people, while also doing his best to take care of the theater, spoke volumes.

Beau said, as if guessing her thoughts, "He's quite a guy, you know. Generous to a fault. He's offered to cover the cost of business and accounting classes at community college, so I can learn the tools of the trade."

"That is generous," Alice said.

"He's incredibly committed. He says he and I will make sure the theater stands for another hundred years."

"I'm surprised he likes Billy Brine. The podcast is turning the tragedy at the Blithedale Theater into sensationalist gossip."

"Maybe he thinks any PR is good PR." Beau shrugged. "Anyway, I'm worried Mr. Gorny is overstretching himself. He's ferrying those kids around, keeping the theater in tip-top shape, and taking care of the farm he lives on. It's a lot. Which is why I'm headed to Dorothy's place now."

"To go through her things?"

"Don't tell Mr. Gorny. I really don't want his help. For his own sake. And honestly, for mine. I'm hoping that going through Dorothy's possessions will give me some kind of closure—or at least a foundation for a fresh start."

Beau said his goodbyes and left Alice to mull over what he'd said.

"If you looked any more thoughtful," Becca said, reappearing at the counter, "you'd be a philosopher. Penny for your thoughts."

"Guess I just worry about what Billy Brine and his followers will find in the woods."

"You're tempted to tag along, aren't you?"

She was. But there was a more urgent matter on her mind. Beau might throw out Dorothy's plans for the theater, and the more she thought of the presentation, the more her instinct told her it must contain something important.

"Alice," Becca said. "What's on your mind? What aren't you telling me?"

Alice shrugged. "Nothing. Everything's fine."

Just imagine, she thought, *if I can recover that presentation and show it to Becca and Ona—then they'll see how much I can contribute.*

CHAPTER 26

*W*ith a security system guarding Dorothy's home, Alice would not be able to break in and find the Future Fund presentation. Under normal circumstances. But since Beau was inside the house, he'd turned off the security system. What better time to slip inside and grab the folder?

As Alice hid in the bushes across the street, she was trying to convince herself of that logic. *See, Beau's even opening windows and doors for you—he's making it easy.*

Beau seemed to be airing out Dorothy's home, pushing all the windows wide open. He even left the front door ajar. She could see him moving around inside, passing a window, vanishing, then reappearing at an upstairs window. He seemed to sit down—maybe on a bed?

Better go now. Who knows how long he'll be upstairs...

She pushed past the bushes, reaching the edge of the street. Her phone buzzed in her pocket. Instinctively, she pulled it out and saw a message from Ona.

Wonderland closed. No sign of you with Billy
and co. So, where are you?

Alice's thumb hovered over the message. She was tempted to write back, tell Ona where she was, get her help. It had felt good to share the investigation with her.

Alice glanced over at the house.

She couldn't waste time. She needed to move now. And again, she thought of how impressed Becca and Ona would be when she recovered Dorothy's Future Fund presentation.

Then I'll involve them more in the investigations.

She pocketed her phone.

Cautiously, she inched up to one of the windows and glanced inside. She could see the dining table covered with folders and paperwork—and beyond it, the living room full of vinyl records and CDs.

She tiptoed over to the front door. It stood ajar, but the opening was too narrow for her to pass through. She tensed as she pushed open the door, expecting it to creak, expecting Beau to come down the stairs and catch her. But the door swung open smoothly, the hinges silent. When she stepped inside, the floorboards didn't groan and give her away, either.

In the front hallway, she stared up the staircase to the second floor.

Something went bump. She listened. Then heard it again. Followed by a loud sigh and the sound of creaking springs—upstairs, Beau must've sat down on that bed again. The rustling of pages told her he must be reading something or going through papers.

What she heard was good news. It meant he was upstairs and might stay there for a while. But it was also bad. Because if she could hear small sounds like rustling upstairs, it wouldn't take much to alert him to her presence downstairs.

She moved toward the doorway. And her phone buzzed again. To Alice, it sounded as loud as a whole hive of angry bees.

Alice?

Alice took another step. Her phone buzzed again.

Stop ignoring me.

Alice switched her phone to Do Not Disturb, so it wouldn't even vibrate. She tiptoed from the hallway into the living room. From there, she moved into the dining room, heading straight for the table with all the documents.

Everything looked the same as before. She couldn't be sure, but she guessed Beau hadn't removed anything yet. That was good. But she'd never have enough time to look through all this stuff, anyway—there were dozens of ring binders, piles of paperwork, and stacks of manila folders.

She opened a red ring binder and flipped through old invoices, and seeing nothing suspicious, quickly closed it. She wasn't even sure what she was looking for.

I'll know it when I see it...

A breeze fluttered the curtains. A car drove down the street, making Alice's heart leap. But to an outsider, the house wouldn't look suspicious at all—not with all the windows open. So she didn't duck or move, and soon the sound of the engine faded.

She flipped through a pile of loose papers. Nothing but utilities bills for Dorothy's home. She turned to a stack of manila folders. The top one contained printouts from the Internet with listings of local folk and bluegrass bands. Among them, Alice saw the Pointed Firs, Blithedale's own bluegrass trio.

She closed the folder and selected the next one, a manila folder, and drew in a sharp breath.

On the cover, in heavy marker pen, it said, "Blithedale Future Fund."

She flipped it open. The first page, a printout, said, "Presentation: The New Blithedale Theater."

This was the presentation Dorothy had planned to give to Alice and her friends at the Blithedale Future Fund meeting the day after her murder. This was it. An electrical current seemed to course through Alice's limbs. Something in this manila folder, her instinct told her, held the key to Dorothy's death.

She reached for the next page.

"Alice," a voice hissed, and she gasped and dropped the folder on the table.

"Alice."

She turned toward the sound. Ona's face was visible in the open window. She was standing outside the house. It must've been her pickup truck that drove past the house.

Ona, frowning, said, "What do you think you're doing?"

Alice put a finger to her lips. Then mouthed the words "he's upstairs."

Ona stepped back from the window. Alice could see her backing into the street, looking upward. She looked back at Alice and shook her head. She mouthed, "I don't see him."

Then Alice heard a sound.

Creaking on the staircase.

He's coming.

Her heart leaped into her throat. Coming down the stairs, he'd see her if she tried to leave through the front door. She'd have to get out the back.

The porch doors—quick!

She spun around, grabbed the folder, and turned to bolt for the back.

Her body went cold.

Beau was standing in the doorway.

"You're not going anywhere…"

CHAPTER 27

*B*eau moved close to Alice. So close, she tried to step back and struck the table behind her. She was trapped.

"You're not going anywhere," he repeated, "until you explain what you're doing here."

"I was just—"

She gripped the manila folder hard, pressing it to her chest.

He saw it.

He reached out, and she didn't see any way she could resist. She was in Dorothy's house—his house—and she was stealing a thing that belonged to him.

He grabbed the manila folder, pulling it out of her hands. He glanced at the cover. A frown gathered on his face.

"What's this? The Blithedale Future Fund…?"

"It's—it's—" Alice's voice shook. But she squared her jaw and took a deep breath to steady herself. "It's a good thing. It's a fund that Becca, Ona, and I run to support local businesses and help revitalize Blithedale."

"I've heard of it." Beau studied her. "And you were going to support the theater? Why?"

"Dorothy asked to be considered. She was going to present this to us—" Alice pointed at the folder in his hands. "—the day after she died."

"You were going to steal it."

"I was going to look at it. I think—"

She cut herself off. How much could she tell Beau? How much *should* she? She'd written him off as a suspect, and yet he stood to gain from Dorothy's death. He stood to gain more than anyone. If the folder contained the key to the mystery and Beau somehow was involved, what should she do?

Beau said, "Yes, what is it you think?"

Alice said nothing.

Beau held the manila folder to his chest. "You knew about this and you didn't tell me. I understand why. You didn't trust me with the information. You thought I wouldn't know what to do with it. And I guess you were right." He sighed. "I've tried to avoid getting more help from others, even Mr. Gorny. He's already helping me so much. I wanted to prove that I could do this on my own—that I'm not the person I used to be."

"It's not that I didn't trust you," Alice said.

"Then why didn't you talk to me? Why didn't you tell me about all this? Why did you break into the house—not just once, but twice?"

Alice looked down at her feet.

"That's right—a neighbor saw you the first time," Beau said.

"I climbed through a window."

Beau stared at her. Finally, he nodded. "All right. You get points for honesty. Who was the guy with you? The neighbor said he saw two people."

"I came alone," she said, suddenly wondering what had happened to Ona. She didn't dare look over at the window, in case it drew Beau's attention. "I caught someone else trying to break in. The wild man in the woods. But I scared him off."

"I can't decide whether to have you arrested," Beau said, a wry smile on his face, "or thank you. Anyway, I'll look through this folder of Dorothy's, and I promise that whatever she planned to do, I will respect it."

That was when she saw Ona. She was tiptoeing into the room, sneaking up on Beau, a baseball bat raised over her head.

Alice raised a hand. "No, it's all right."

Beau turned and let out a yelp—and stumbled backward.

"I'm all right," Alice assured Ona, who lowered the baseball bat.

A phone buzzed. Alice reached for hers, then remembered that she'd switched the vibration off. Beau dug his out, looked at the screen, and then answered.

"Mr. Gorny…I'm at Dorothy's…I know, but I wanted to… I mean, you're welcome to come over…" Then his eyebrows shot up in surprise. "He what?!"

Beau lowered the phone.

"It's Billy Brine," he said.

"Billy Brine?" Alice asked. "What did he do now?"

"He's been attacked. By the wild man in the woods."

CHAPTER 28

Ona's pickup truck bounced down the deeply rutted dirt road. The road grew narrower, until it turned into a track too narrow to drive on, and coming upon another pickup truck parked by an enormous tree, Beau, Ona, and Alice jumped out.

"That's Mr. Gorny's truck," Beau said.

They continued on foot. The massive trees around them stood as still and silent as stone statues. A crow squawked. Alice felt abnormally cold, as if a cold breeze kept blowing down her spine. Yet the wind was still, the air mild.

The track turned and then dipped into a gully. At the bottom, the young people stood in a cluster, including the two girls with purple hair. At the center lay Billy Brine. He had his back against a big, moss-covered rock. Mr. Gorny was helping him to his feet. Or to one foot, rather. Billy bent as he winced, trying to keep his weight off the other foot.

As Alice, Ona, and Beau approached, Billy looked up.

"I saw him," he said, triumphantly. "I saw Arthur Crumpit. I recognized him at once, despite the long hair and beard."

Mr. Gorny wrapped an arm around the young man's back

and helped him to hobble toward the dirt track. Billy winced again.

When he caught sight of Beau, Mr. Gorny stopped. He frowned.

"We agreed you'd wait to go through Dorothy's things."

"I thought you'd appreciate—"

Mr. Gorny held up a hand. "What I'd appreciate is this: If it's theater business, you and I should discuss it privately." He glanced at Alice and Ona. Then back at Beau. "The two of us."

"Sure thing, Mr. Gorny."

Beau's open, honest—almost naïve—look of gratitude toward his benefactor made Alice wonder. How good a judge of character was Mr. Gorny? He seemed to admire Billy Brine, which wasn't promising. So, did he really understand Beau's ability to run the theater? Or was he blinded by his commitment to the Bowers family tradition?

She watched Mr. Gorny support Billy up the track, with Beau tagging along. A few paces behind them came the young followers. Except the two girls with purple hair. They stayed behind, joining Alice and Ona in observing the crowd disappear over the ridge by the gully.

One of the girls said, "It's strange…"

Alice glanced at her. The girl continued to look up at where the others had vanished over the hill and into the trees.

"What's strange?"

"The wild man."

"You saw him?"

"No, that's what's strange. I didn't."

"Me, too," the other girl said. "I mean, I didn't see him, either. We saw Billy, though. He didn't know we were down in the gully."

"Billy was up there," the first said, turning and pointing at a cliff jutting out over the gully.

"Yeah," the other said. "Right up there on the cliff."

"And he looked around, like he was trying to see who was there."

"Then he fell."

Alice said, "He fell? You mean the wild man pushed him?"

"There was no wild man. Billy just fell. Like—"

The two purple-haired girls exchanged a look.

One of them bit her lip. Then said, "Like, he let himself fall."

CHAPTER 29

On Monday morning, the sun had just risen over the green hills of Blithedale, when Becca and Ona walked into Wonderland Books. They shut the red door behind them.

"What's going on?" Alice asked, surprised.

Surprised to see Becca away from the diner. Surprised by the closed door. And surprised by the grave looks they gave her.

Becca pointed to a bench. "Sit."

"Becca, Ona, is this—"

"Sit."

Alice shut her mouth. Becca's tone brooked no argument. She did as she was told, coming out from behind the counter. She sat down.

Becca sat across from her, Ona next to her.

Alice had a flashback to a conversation with her aunt and uncle—something about a school report—and it made her skin crawl.

Except her aunt and uncle probably hadn't brought coffee. Becca reached into a tote bag for a thermos and mugs, pouring the coffee and handing out the mugs to Alice and Ona.

"We need to talk," Becca said.

"Uh," Alice said. "OK."

"Something is keeping you from talking to us. From sharing your thoughts and questions and concerns. And we want to understand why. Is something the matter?"

"Nothing's the matter." Alice sipped her coffee, avoiding eye contact. "Nothing."

Becca nodded. "Then why are you—"

Ona cut her off. "Then why are you ignoring my messages? Why are you lying and sneaking around?" She spoke with rising intensity, but then dropped to a whisper. "And why are you pretending it doesn't hurt us when you do that?"

Alice stared, wide-eyed, at her friend. "I didn't know—"

Her voice rose again. "How would you like it if we ignored you? How would you like it if we kept secrets from you?"

"I didn't mean to—"

"We live together—in the same town, in the same old house—and yet you treat me like a stranger. Didn't you think I'd notice? Didn't you think I'd care?"

"Of course, I think you care," Alice said, heat rising to her face, shame mixing with anger. "If you'll let me explain—"

"I get it," Ona said, crossing her arms. "You want to do everything yourself. Without us."

"That's not true," Alice snapped.

There was a long awkward silence. Ona, arms still crossed, looked away, frowning. Though Alice feared she was trying to hide her true emotion: hurt.

Then Becca said, "It is true, honey. Lately, you've been flying solo, and despite our best efforts, you've pushed us away again and again."

Alice felt emotion rising like pressure, her gauge pressing into red.

"I just wanted time and space."

"To do what?"

"To prove I can do it."

"Do what, honey? What is it you need to prove you can do?"

"Anything," she cried out. "Everything."

She put down her coffee mug. She wiped a hand across her eyes, surprised to feel wetness on her face. She was crying.

Becca got up from her seat and went to sit on the other side of Alice. "But, sweetie, who can do everything? And who would ever ask a friend to do so much? Not me."

"And not me," Ona said, turning back to Alice.

"I just want to—" Alice let out a sob, and forced the next one back. "I just want to contribute."

Her eyes blurred. She felt Becca's arm around her. Then Ona's.

"You do contribute," Becca said. "You contribute plenty."

"But how? I depend on charity to run my shop."

"A loan, honey. A loan."

"People give me books. Ona, you gave me this entire house, for crying out loud. And then what do I do? I live rent free at your inn, like some kind of deadbeat friend you can't get off your couch."

She drew in a ragged breath.

"I thought I could pay you back—pay Blithedale back—by helping Dorothy and the theater take a step toward its rebirth, like you did for me. But the whole thing became a mess. My mess to clean up."

Ona said, "But Alice, you didn't kill Dorothy. And you didn't mismanage the Blithedale Theater as a business. It was never your mess to clean up."

"And what's this about paying back?" Becca said. "Yes, you have a loan to pay back. But otherwise, you don't owe anyone anything."

"But the tiny house you made, Ona…"

"I made because I compulsively build tiny houses," Ona said. "I would've built one anyway, and it gave me so much pleasure to create one I knew you'd appreciate. It was as much a gift to me as it was to you."

"But then I don't even pay rent."

"At my invitation. If I needed that rent, I'd ask for it. Or kick you out on the street."

She nudged Alice playfully.

"But the truth is, I won't do that. You know why?"

Alice shook her head.

"Because I love having you at the inn. I spend my days seeing people come and people go. You'd think that wouldn't get lonely, but it does. It's a comfort to me to have a dear friend living in the Colonel Brandon suite. You think I'm doing you a favor. Sure, I am. But did you ever consider my needs in all this?"

Alice was silent. She hadn't, of course, and now, looking at Ona's earnest expression, she realized how little she knew about what her friend really felt about the situation. Not just her, Alice's, situation—but *their* situation.

Ona, her arm wrapped around Alice's back, gave her a squeeze. Becca did too. And for a while, they sat in silence. Their warmth mingled with hers and she felt safer, more at peace than she had in a long time. Why had she pushed this warmth away? Why had she pushed her friends away?

"I'm sorry," she said.

Becca said, "This whole contribution thing. What's it really about?"

Alice drew in a deep breath and exhaled.

Then, beginning with the aftermath of her mom's death,

she told them the story of life with her aunt and uncle, and how little Alice had worked so hard to contribute—to prove that she wasn't a burden to her guardians. And as she told her story, her friends expressed their outrage, their sorrow, and their admiration for the little girl.

"You must've felt so alone," Ona said.

"Well," Becca said, tightening her arm around Alice. "You're not alone anymore."

A knock at the door made all three of them jump, and they looked at each other with surprise. Then, the tension from all the emotion suddenly broken, Alice burst into laughter. Then Ona did, too. And finally Becca joined them.

"I love you, ladies," Alice said. "Now, let's see who's at the door."

CHAPTER 30

"*I* thought you planned to throw it all away."

"I changed my mind." Beau Bowers tapped the manila folder. "*This* changed my mind."

He smiled, though he looked exhausted. Dark circles ringed his eyes. As Alice handed him a mug of coffee, he explained that he'd been up half the night reading Dorothy's plans for the Blithedale Theater—and now he was eager to share it with them.

Alice glanced at the manila folder in his hands.

"It doesn't look like it would take so long to read," she said.

"Oh, it wasn't her presentation that took time. It was understanding how she'd figured it all out." He sighed. "I've spent most of my life driving in the dark without my headlights on. Now that I'm sober, I want to see—and see clearly. It wasn't enough to read the plans that Dorothy was going to present to you all. I wanted to understand how she'd made the plans—and what the implications for the family business would be."

Alice recalled the dining table covered in documents, and

could imagine Beau sitting at that table until late at night, trawling through brochures and invoices, trying to make sense of it all.

"So?" Ona said, impatiently. "You can't give us all this build-up without telling us what the plans are."

"Fair enough," Beau said, smiling. "Here goes."

Alice, Becca, and Ona got comfortable on the little benches in Wonderland Books, sitting close together, as Beau began his presentation—Dorothy's presentation—for the Future Fund.

It began with a long preamble on the history of the Blithedale Theater—its early success on the Vaudeville circuit, and how the Bowers family had soon prospered. The hard times of the Depression, a brush with bankruptcy around World War II, and then a phoenix-like rebirth from the ashes, as the theater doubled down on movies. The good times lasted decades before the home video revolution threatened the theater's existence. Still, the Bowers struggled on. Until multiplexes and digital projectors and home streaming services arrived, and fewer and fewer people came to watch old movies on the big screen.

"Of course, we can't blame the new technology," Beau said, "since we never ditched the old. My parents stubbornly refused to convert to digital. Running a 35mm movie theater in the 21st century may seem quaint. It's actually a recipe for disaster."

He shared the theater's financials. They were nothing but doom and gloom—Dorothy had kept meticulous records and, as Beau said, she was nobody's fool.

"She saw the writing on the wall. The question was not whether the Blithedale Theater would have to close. The question was when."

Alice, Becca, and Ona exchanged glances. Alice knew they were all thinking the same thing: *I had no idea it was so bad.*

"So Dorothy came up with a plan," Beau continued. "But she needed startup funding."

"That's where the Blithedale Fund came in," Alice said.

"It was lucky timing. You reached out about supporting the theater, right when she was ready to begin—ready to transform it."

"Transform it?" Becca let out a sigh. "Well, transform it into what? You've delayed the big reveal long enough, don't you think?"

Beau smiled. "You're right."

He dug into the manila folder. The papers he unfolded— careful not to tear it at the seams—turned out to be a glossy poster. He held it up and grinned, clearly proud.

"Wow," Ona said.

"It's beautiful," Becca said.

Alice leaned forward, resting her chin on one hand as she studied the poster. Dorothy had paid an illustrator to create a drawing of the Blithedale Theater. It showed the outside and, as if the beholder had x-ray vision, it offered a circular view of the lobby and another of the auditorium.

The marquee outside remained the same, retaining the classic old theater look. But the lobby was transformed. A classy bar and lounge area had replaced the concession stand. The auditorium showed every seat occupied and, on stage, a band playing.

"Music," Alice said. "Dorothy wanted to turn the theater into a music venue."

Beau lowered the poster. "Music, comedy, even a little theater. Even a music school for adults and kids." He pointed out practice rooms in the basement. "The movie business was a bust. Why compete with the multiplexes or streaming services? Instead, the Bowers family theater would return to its roots: the performance arts." He sighed. "Judging by her notes, she was over-the-moon excited about the plans, and couldn't wait to share it with the world."

"She did hint at it," Alice said. "She talked to Althea."

Ona said, "That's right. She offered the Pointed Firs a gig, and no one believed Althea and the bluegrass ladies."

"Everyone's so used to the theater showing movies," Becca said. "But I tell you, everyone's going to be thrilled when this happens."

"Well, I'm sure not everyone," Beau said. "When I called Mr. Gorny this morning and told him about it, he got upset. He's committed to the old movie theater concept. But there's no future in it." He looked at each of them in turn. "I believe in Dorothy's plans. They're perfect for Blithedale. But it'll take a lot of hard work and money. I know I can't do this on my own. I need everyone's help—not just Mr. Gorny's but all of Blithedale's. And I was hoping the Future Fund would still consider supporting the theater…"

Alice, Ona, and Becca, looked at each other.

Alice said, "Well, ladies, what do you think?"

"No brainer," Becca said.

"Clear winner," Ona agreed.

She looked at her friends for another moment, making sure they weren't simply saying so to please her. But she could tell they were as enthusiastic about the plans as she was.

Finally, she said, "Then I agree, too."

A huge weight lifted off her shoulders, a weight she realized she'd been carrying ever since she secretly invited Dorothy to submit her plans to the Future Fund without Becca and Ona's knowledge.

She let out a long breath.

Things would be all right.

Then she heard sirens.

CHAPTER 31

Outside in the street, a police cruiser drove past with its lights flashing. Through the open car window, Alice caught sight of Chief Jimbo, his face pinched with worry.

Alice closed the door to her bookstore and locked it. She looked at her friends.

"Let's go see what's going on," she said.

Together, they set off. Beau followed them. So did others in the street.

Maybe because emotions had run high in the bookstore, she felt the air was charged with a sense of foreboding, as if a storm was coming. Or maybe her instincts really were right. Maybe they were on the brink of solving the mystery.

The three of them jogged down the street, following the direction of Chief Jimbo's cruiser. They didn't have to go far. The cruiser stood parked at the curb outside Love Again, Esther's consignment store. Alice, Becca, and Ona burst inside, and Chief Jimbo jumped, visibly startled, and dropped his notepad and pencil on the floor. He stooped to pick them up.

"What happened?" Alice asked. "Are you all right, Esther?"

Esther shook her head with a frown. "I'm fine. But there's been a theft."

"Oh."

"Yes, *oh*. People do steal from my store." She gave a shrug. "I'm sure it's the same at your bookstore."

Alice thankfully hadn't experienced it yet, but she knew it was only a matter of time. Beau and others stood in the doorway, looking around, as if they expected to see all the merchandise gone.

"It's what they stole that's upsetting," Esther said.

She pointed over at a low shelf. A row of shoes stood neatly lined up. In the middle of the row of shoes there was an empty space, apparently where a pair had gone missing. Alice's gut twisted. She knew at once which shoes were gone.

"No," she said, and put a hand to her mouth.

"Yes," Esther said grimly. "The ruby-red sneakers."

Ona drew in a sharp breath of air. She put a hand on Alice's arm.

"What do you think it means?"

"I think it means the killer intends to strike again. If only we knew who stole the shoes."

Esther said, "Oh, I know who stole them."

Alice, Becca, Ona, and Chief Jimbo stared at her, all equally surprised.

"Well, I saw him," Esther said. "Long hair and grubby clothes. He grabbed the shoes and bolted, hobbling out of the store before I could grab him."

"The wild man," Alice said.

"That's right," Esther said with a grimace. "The wild man of the woods."

CHAPTER 32

"*T*his isn't good," Chief Jimbo said.

Alice, Becca, and Ona stood outside the consignment store. Chief Jimbo leaned against his cruiser and mopped his brow with a wad of takeout napkins. It wasn't a hot day, yet he was sweating profusely.

"There'll be another murder, for sure," he said.

"Maybe the wild man had another reason for stealing those shoes," Ona said. "Like he needs a pair of decent sneakers."

"Well, there were other, less conspicuous shoes," Alice said.

Ona tapped her eye patch with its glittering rhinestones. "Just because you live alone in the woods doesn't mean you don't like a little sparkle."

"No, no," Chief Jimbo said. "It's not the missing shoes that worry me. It's that I got another call warning me about the Oz Killer."

Alice frowned. "'Another call'? What do you mean, 'another call'?"

Chief Jimbo colored. "Uh…"

"Jimbo," Ona said. "You'd better come clean."

He reached into his cruiser and rooted around in a brown paper bag from a burger joint and brought out more napkins to mop the back of his neck with. It seemed to Alice he was stalling.

"Jimbo," Becca said, giving him her most sympathetic look. "You can tell us the truth. What's this about a call?"

He sighed, his shoulder slumping. He seemed to grow an inch shorter.

"I got a call after Dorothy died with information about the Oz Killer. About the ruby-red sneakers. The connection to the previous murders. Everything I needed to—" He looked down at his shoes. He mumbled, "Everything I needed to solve the case."

Ona gave Alice a raised eyebrow, a look that said, *Good grief.*

"I really wanted to—to—to—"

He shook his head, and for a moment, Alice wondered whether he was going to burst into tears. She realized what he was going to say: "I really wanted to solve the case."

Becca apparently did, too. She put an arm around Jimbo's shoulders.

"It's all right," she said.

Nobody in town took Chief Jimbo seriously. His father had been Blithedale's sole cop before his son took over, and everyone remembered Chief Sapling, Sr. as being highly competent. They weren't easy shoes for young Jimbo to fill.

"Who called you?" Alice asked, speaking gently.

"I don't know. It was anonymous."

"A hidden number?"

He shook his head. "I'm guessing from a pay phone. I tried calling back. No answer."

"Let's try again."

Chief Jimbo dug out his cell phone and scrolled through

the list of incoming calls. Then stopped when he found the right one. He put on the speaker and pressed call. It rang and rang and rang. Eventually, when no one answered, the call dropped.

"Lower the volume on your phone," Alice said. "But keep calling. I want to listen."

Chief Jimbo did as she asked him to. Alice moved away from him until she couldn't hear the sound from his phone, hoping to hear the distant ringing of a phone.

"Nothing," she said. She turned to Ona, who shook her head, too.

"Where are there pay phones in town?" Alice asked.

"Most are gone," Chief Jimbo said. "But there is one at the public library."

"And the diner," Becca said. "I'll go check it."

Alice and Ona piled into Chief Jimbo's cruiser to go to the public library. It smelled of hamburger and french fries, and Alice chose to sit in the backseat with Ona, because it was considerably cleaner than the passenger's side—a dumping ground for potato chip bags, empty soda cans, and crumpled up lottery tickets.

The cruiser drifted down Main Street, heading toward the public library. As they got out, Alice was relieved to gulp in fresh air. The cruiser smelled like a teenage boy's bedroom.

Becca messaged her:

> Back at the diner. By our pay phone. Try
> calling now.

Alice told Chief Jimbo to call, and he let it ring and ring.

> Nope. Not ringing.

Ona led the way, pushing open the doors to the public

library, and Lorraine, behind the circulation desk, gave the three of them a startled look.

"Is there a fire somewhere?"

"Do you have a public pay phone?"

She nodded at one off to the side of the entrance.

Chief Jimbo called the number again.

A phone rang. Everyone jumped.

But it wasn't the pay phone. It was Alice's phone.

CHAPTER 33

"*J* found the wild man in the woods." Beau spoke breathlessly on the phone, as if he'd been running. "I was heading home and saw him passing the road. I decided to stop. And I followed him through the forest, and there he was, camping at the Natty Bumppo Falls."

"Beau—" Alice said, trying to cut him off.

"He's built a lean-to against the cliff to hide a tent, and he's got a tarp strung between four trees, giving him a dry outdoor space, too. And then he saw me and I ran—"

"Beau, you've got to listen to me."

"I'm so excited. It's like catching sight of a celebrity or Santa." He laughed. "So, Alice, what's up?"

"Something's wrong. It seems the wild man stole the last pair of ruby-red sneakers. It may be a sign that he's involved in Dorothy's murder."

"Hold on, Alice. Someone's at the door."

"Beau—no, wait!"

But he was gone. He'd put down his phone without hanging up. She heard his footsteps and the creaking of his cabin floor and then the door.

Speaking. Beau's voice—and another's. A man's angry voice spiking above Beau's, and then—

Crash!

Beau screamed. "No, no, no—"

"The phone," someone growled. "Switch off the phone."

Alice gasped.

The phone went dead.

"What?" Ona asked.

"Quick," Alice said. "Into the cruiser."

Ona didn't hesitate. She jumped into the back of the police cruiser with Alice. Once in the driver's seat, Chief Jimbo, looking in the rearview mirror, gave Alice a confused look.

"What's going on?"

"Drive," she barked. "I'll tell you on the way."

Chief Jimbo turned on the engine and put the car in drive. But didn't drive. He turned to her.

"Should I, uh—" He swallowed. "—use the siren?"

"Yes!"

He switched on the flashing lights and the siren and, gripping the steering wheel so hard that his knuckles turned white, accelerated down Main Street. Pedestrians stopped and stared. Chief Jimbo never used the siren. Now he'd used it twice today. And even as they drove, Alice could tell how the sound seemed to make him shrink in his seat.

He's more scared of police sirens than any criminal would be.

She didn't know whether to feel exasperated or sympathetic. But as she watched Chief Jimbo sweat and grind his teeth, she settled on sympathy. It was painful to watch someone so unsuited to their job.

"You're doing great," she said, placing a hand gently on his shoulder.

"What's going on?" Ona asked.

Alice told them what had happened on the phone, and how it had sounded as if someone had attacked Beau.

"It's the wild man of the woods, isn't it?" Ona said. "Beau found him, so the wild man went after him."

"Maybe…"

Alice couldn't make it all fit. The wild man stealing the shoes. Beau discovering his hiding place. The attack at home. There was a kind of logic to all that. But how did it fit with Dorothy's death? If the Oz Killer wasn't real, and there wasn't a madman out there arbitrarily targeting women named Dorothy, then what motive did the wild man have? Who was he? What did he want?

She shook her head. Whatever the truth was, it could wait —they needed to get to Beau as quickly as possible.

Chief Jimbo proved to be a better driver than he was an investigator. They flew up the road and drove deeper and deeper into the woods, then swerved onto the rutted track that led past Beau's cabin, bumping and shaking so wildly that Alice thought her head was going to pop off.

Chief Jimbo hit the brakes and they skidded to a stop.

In an instant, the three of them were out of the car and racing toward the cabin in the clearing. In the distance, Alice thought she heard the sound of a car roaring as it sped away, heading down the dirt road and disappearing deeper into the woods.

But if someone was escaping, they couldn't give chase. Their first priority had to be Beau. And the cabin door, ominously, stood ajar.

"Your gun," Ona whispered to Chief Jimbo.

"My gun?" he asked.

"Get it out."

"Oh, right." He fumbled with his holster, finally managing to pull his gun. "There."

Alice, feeling no more confident with Chief Jimbo holding a gun, pushed open the door.

Beau lay in the middle of the cabin on his back. His feet had been half squeezed into the pair of red sneakers, his heels sticking out.

"No."

Alice rushed forward and threw herself on her knees. Blood oozed from the back of Beau's head, where he'd been clobbered. She put a hand on his chest. Ona got down on her knees, too, and checked the pulse on his wrist.

"He's alive," she said.

"And breathing," Alice said. "But we need to get him to a hospital quick."

Carefully, Alice and Ona lifted Beau. Chief Jimbo stood by the door, gaping, his gun hand hanging limply by his side.

"Come on, Jimbo," Ona said. "Go open the car so we can get Beau inside."

"Uh, right away."

Outside, Chief Jimbo opened the back of his cruiser, and gently, Alice and Ona laid Beau on the back seat. Alice slipped into the back, putting Beau's head in her lap. It was sticky with blood. Ona got in the passenger seat, cursing as she pushed aside food wrappers and empty soda cans.

"Come on, Jimbo. Pedal to the metal."

Chief Jimbo nodded. He swung the cruiser around, executing a three-point turn so smoothly that Alice was sure a driving instructor would've given him a medal. Then they were roaring down the rutted road, the siren blaring.

Beau groaned.

Alice took his hand.

"You're going to be all right," she said.

She hoped she wasn't telling a lie. Beau had seemed to get a second chance—a life free from alcohol, a fresh start. It seemed especially cruel that it should end now. Also, he'd seen his attacker. Beau must know who the killer was.

But he was out cold now, only occasionally drifting toward consciousness when they hit a big bump, and then he'd groan or mutter something unintelligible.

"Look out!"

Chief Jimbo hit the brakes, and Alice and Beau flew forward. She pressed her feet into the floor and clung to him, barely keeping them from smashing into the seats in front of them.

Alice looked up. "Hey, careful!"

Chief Jimbo pointed out the windshield. Alice craned her neck to see.

In the middle of the dirt road ahead of the cruiser, caught like a deer in headlights, stood a tall, gangly man with long ragged hair and a beard. He stared at them with wild eyes. Then he bolted into the woods.

Alice gaped, her heart pounding. The wild man of the woods. Who was this stranger? Those eyes…she'd seen those eyes before.

She made a split decision.

She eased Beau back on the seat and opened the car door.

Ona turned in her seat. "What're you doing?"

"I'm going to get some answers," Alice said. "I'm going to catch that wild man."

CHAPTER 34

*T*he wild man fled through the woods, and Alice followed.

She caught flashes of him through the trees. A long-haired, long-legged man in a green jacket, which made him more and more difficult to see as the vegetation grew denser.

He crested a hill and looked back. Then vanished down the other side.

By the time she'd reached the top and could look down at a gully below—one with a creek running through it—he was gone.

She scanned the terrain. He could be hiding behind a tree. Or he could be a mile away, running as fast as those long legs would carry him. She listened. A bird fluttered from its perch. Water burbled in the fast-flowing creek. But no sounds indicated a wild man thrashing through the undergrowth.

She walked down the hill, trying to control her disappointment.

Now what? Where did he go?

A car had sped away from the cabin. But the wild man had moved with confidence through the woods—on foot. Would he have attacked Beau, then fled in a car, only to reappear on foot? That made no sense.

Coming to the creek, she crouched down and put a hand in the water. She breathed deeply. The quiet of the woods settled over her. Once again, she'd run off alone. She hadn't even paused to consider that she might be better off with Ona by her side, but now she felt it—alone and vulnerable.

She was beginning to see that it was one thing to recognize behavior that had served her well in the past, but which she no longer needed to the same extent, and quite another to correct it.

Next time, I'll do better. Maybe not perfect. But better.

Meanwhile, she was alone in the woods, chasing a man who might be a murderer.

Again, she tried to think of where the guy might be.

The icy coldness in the creek bore down on her with unexpected strength. As she lifted her hand out, she had an idea. Something must be driving the water downward.

She looked up the creek. Where had Beau said he'd found the wild man's camp? The Natty Bumppo Falls. She didn't know where that was, but she had a hunch.

She stood up and headed up the creek, careful to scan the woods now and then for any signs of the wild man. But apart from nature's constant cracks, creaks, and chatter, the forest was quiet.

She clambered over massive tree roots and stepped carefully over rocks.

As the terrain rose, the creek got swifter and swifter. It pushed through larger and larger rocks until she was scrambling over boulders to follow the path of the water. She grabbed a boulder and pulled herself up and saw, as she reached the top, the ground flattening above.

Up here, the creek crossed a plateau, and the sound of crashing water was far louder. Because a hundred feet away, a cliff wall rose from the forest floor, and water gushed out from the top.

"The Natty Bumppo Falls," Alice said.

"Falls" made it sound grand. Actually, the little creek cascaded over a cliff and flowed across the level ground before plummeting onto the boulder-filled gully beneath. Regardless of its grandeur, the idyllic scene would have impressed her if her focus wasn't on what else lay on the plateau.

A lean-to stood against the cliff wall about twenty feet to the right of the falls. Under the lean-to stood a small tent. Nearby, a tarp had stretched between four trees, high enough up to provide shelter from rain, yet not interfere with a campfire placed below.

The wild man's camp—exactly as Beau had described it.

She approached the tent with caution. Her heart thudded in her chest. Every few steps, she glanced over her shoulders, convinced she'd see the wild man come rushing at her.

But all was quiet.

She found the tent opening zipped closed. Crouching down, she eased it open, and then clenched her jaw at the zipping sound. She pulled the tent flap open and peered inside.

The tent was empty.

Or rather, there was no one inside. It wasn't empty. The wild man had crammed it full of things. An old, battered laptop. A pile of papers. Books. Bottles. Wadded-up napkins. And a large sealed crate.

She undid the clasps on the crate. Inside, there was food. A loaf of bread. Canned beans and fruit. A bag of tortilla chips and a jar of salsa. Hard cheese. A packet of ham. Mayo.

Next to the crate lay three bottles. Red wine and bourbon.

What had Sandy said the thief had taken from her house? A special bottle of bourbon she'd gotten as a gift. So it was true—it had been the wild man who'd raided her larder and fridge.

Alice turned her attention to the mess of papers and books.

Profiling Serial Killers: A Practical Guide.

101 Unsolved Murders.

But also, interestingly, Frank L. Baum's *The Wonderful Wizard of Oz.*

The papers were printouts off the Internet—articles describing Dorothy's murder, the Oz Killer, theories about Arthur Crumpit. But also lots of information about the Blithedale Theater and its history, a few mentions of the Bowers family, and several sheets related to Billy Brine.

She opened the laptop. But it was locked, and after trying simple passwords like "1234," she gave up. However, she did notice that the user name was "TT."

Then she saw something red glittering among a pile of dirty clothes. She dug them out. A pair of glittery ruby-red sneakers, big enough to fit a giant.

Sandy's missing shoes...

Sandy had been right—the wild man had stolen them.

Leaving the tent, she wandered around the little camp. Judging by the campfire and how worn down the ground was on the plateau, she guessed the wild man had been camping here for a while.

With her hands on her hips, she surveyed the camp.

"Who are you, wild man?" She looked around, as if the place itself might answer her question. "And where are you?"

She supposed she could wait for him to come back. But the idea of being discovered alone at this camp made her shudder. If he was the one who had attacked Beau, she wouldn't be safe.

So she retraced her steps, climbing down the boulders and following the creek through the gully. She guessed where she'd come down the ridge and made her way back through the woods.

As she walked, she disturbed a deer, who raised her head, alarmed, and then bounded away, disappearing with a flash of her white tail.

It would be easy to lose your way out here. The wild man must know these woods well. She thought of the theory that Arthur Crumpit was the wild man and he'd been living out here for many years. That would explain why he was so familiar with the woods.

But if Crumpit had lived out here for years, people would've spotted him years ago. Hunters, Hikers. Leaf peepers. Someone would've seen him.

No, she didn't believe the wild man was Arthur Crumpit, anymore than she believed that the Oz Killer had murdered Dorothy.

As she approached Beau's cabin again, she was aware that her thoughts were leading her in circles. Whoever the wild man was, it was someone who knew the area well. He'd broken into people's homes to get food. But he'd also broken into the library to get information.

Not to kill people. But to get information...

The contents of the wild man's tent had underscored this —his primary interest seemed to be to gather information. It was like he was investigating.

She opened the door to the cabin, thinking she herself might do a little snooping around while she had the chance. She stepped inside.

There was the pool of blood on the floor, where she'd found Beau. In the panic of finding him, she hadn't noticed this: drops of blood leaving a trail across the floor...

The door slammed shut behind her, and she whirled around.

And there he stood, blocking her exit.

Long-haired, gangly, and red-eyed.

The wild man of the woods.

CHAPTER 35

The wild man broke into a grin.

"Alice," he said. "Good to see you again."

Alice blinked. It couldn't be. She blinked again. But yes—she pictured his hair shorter and his face cleaner. If he'd been wearing a button-down or flannel shirt instead, she would've recognized him at once.

"Todd Townsend," she said.

He inclined his head. "At your service."

"But after your brother got locked up, I thought you—"

"Disappeared? I did. But after Darrell got himself locked up and *The Blithedale Record* folded, I didn't flee to Belize, if that's what you thought. I stayed close to home. I stuck to a camping ground a few towns away. Far enough that people didn't know me. But close enough that I could consider my options."

He sighed.

"I like Blithedale. I loved my newspaper. After my brother was found guilty, I had to shut it down. After all, he was my biggest sponsor. And even though a judge cleared me of any wrongdoing, I didn't feel welcome in town."

"I can't imagine why…"

"You're entitled to your sarcasm. I know I made a mess of things. Which is why I came back." He crossed the room and went to the little kitchen and rummaged through the box of dry foods Beau had left there. He found a jar of instant coffee. "Want some?"

Alice shook her head.

While Todd made himself a cup of coffee, he continued to talk in a relaxed, familiar way, as if they were old friends. Alice hardly knew what to make of it. Darrell Townsend had turned out to be crooked—he was serving a prison sentence to pay for his crimes—but although Todd wasn't convicted of a crime, everyone in town knew that Todd had helped Darrell spread lies via his newspaper, *The Blithedale Record*.

One clue ought to have tipped her off to who the wild man was—he'd made a call to the Winnemac penitentiary. That was where Darrell was incarcerated. And now that she considered how interested the wild man had seemed in the case—as if he were investigating—she could see how it made sense that it was Blithedale's own disgraced journalist who was hiding in the woods.

"I saw Dorothy's death as an opportunity," Todd was saying.

Alice crossed her arms. "This sounds more like the Todd I know."

"An opportunity to do some good."

He'd boiled water in a pot and poured it into a mug with the instant coffee, and now he leaned against the kitchen counter as he blew at the hot drink before sipping it.

"The kind of good you did with your brother?" Alice asked.

He shook his head. "The kind of good that would convince the people of Blithedale that I could be trusted."

Alice laughed. "Funny way to show you can be trusted.

Breaking into people's homes and the public library and the consignment store—"

"I didn't break into the consignment store."

They looked at each other. She believed him.

"All right," Alice said. "Tell me what you know."

Todd smiled. "With pleasure."

He explained how he had seen Dorothy's murder as an opportunity to solve a big case and redeem himself as a journalist. To prove his worth. He'd been investigating the murder while trying to keep out of sight—hence the camp in the woods, the break-ins, the constant running away to hide his identity.

All the while Alice was thinking that if Todd had only come out in the open, if he hadn't played the lone wolf, he might've shared important insights and they could've solved the case sooner.

But then the same could be said of me...

Todd said, "I wanted to expose the killer in a news story and only then reveal my identity."

"You were hoping people would thank you."

He shrugged. "What else could I do?"

Alice sighed. "Well, you could've apologized to people. You could've owned up to the bad things you did and showed us all that you regretted your behavior."

Todd stared at her. Then laughed.

"Oh, come on. This isn't a daytime soap. The world doesn't work like that."

But it works by hiding in the woods, breaking into people's homes, and pretending to be a kind of Big Foot character?

Alice shook her head. A sound made her turn toward the window. Probably just an animal in the woods.

She focused her attention on Todd. She had the feeling he'd rather scale a massive mountain than say the simple words, *I'm sorry*. For some people, saying sorry was more painful than any physical hardship.

Todd sipped his coffee, a self-satisfied look on his face.

"Besides, I'm one step away from solving the case. I've followed the clues, and—"

The cabin door burst open. Todd, startled, dropped his cup of coffee as Becca and Ona barged in. Ona raised the baseball bat she apparently kept in her pickup. Becca clenched her fists.

"Get away from her," Becca said.

Alice couldn't help but smile. She loved these ladies with all their pluck.

"Gee, Becca," Todd said, grinning. "You made me spill."

Becca gaped. "Todd?"

But while Becca and Ona reacted to seeing Todd, Alice's attention was drawn again to the drops of blood on the floor. She examined them closer. They led from the pool of blood to a pile of books and papers stacked against the back wall. She crouched down. A manila folder lay on top of the pile, a bloody smear across the front.

"What's that?" Ona asked over her shoulder

As Alice opened the folder, she realized what it was. The last piece of the puzzle. The papers inside said, "Last Will & Testament." She flipped through the pages. According to the document, Beau would leave the theater business, upon his death, to one William Brine.

"Beau names Billy Brine in his will?" Todd said, craning over her other shoulder to see.

Alice said, "There's literally blood on the document. I'm going to guess Beau didn't do it willingly."

"The killer got sloppy."

"Not a single killer," Alice said. "But killers. Plural."

Beau and two witnesses had signed the last page. Beau's signature was first—in a shaky hand. The scrawl that followed was hard to read, after which came one that was much sloppier. Even so, she could guess whose names they were.

"Gorny," Alice said, pointing to the first. "And Brine."

"Partners in crime," Todd said.

CHAPTER 36

*T*he doors to the Blithedale Theater were unlocked. Inside the lobby, a refrigerator behind the concession stand hummed. As Chief Jimbo, Alice, and Todd passed through, their footfall softened by the thick carpeting, everything was very still. The movie posters on the walls. The gumball machine. The old phone booth. All frozen in time.

Alice put a hand on Chief Jimbo's arm, stopping him.

"Try that number now."

Chief Jimbo dug out his cell phone and called the number of the anonymous informant who'd suggested the Oz Killer had murdered Dorothy. A second after he hit dial, the pay phone in the booth rang.

Chief Jimbo jumped, startled.

"The killer called from here…"

Alice nodded. "*Foolhardy* might be the word he himself would use. But he didn't think you would trace it back to him."

"He emphasized I had a moral obligation to keep his call a secret," Chief Jimbo said and sighed. "He said it was what the old chief of police—my dad—would've done, and he sounded so competent. I believed him."

They moved farther into the lobby, and as they came to the auditorium doors, they heard the muffled sound of music inside. Alice pushed open one of the doors.

The auditorium lights were off. But the projector and speakers were on, a movie showing on the big screen. It was *The Wizard of Oz*. The Munchkins were urging Dorothy to "Follow the Yellow Brick Road, Follow the Yellow Brick Road…" And as Alice, Todd, and Chief Jimbo walked down the dark aisle between the rows of seats, the Munchkins sang, "You're off to see the wizard…"

Alice was aware of how exposed they were. In the glare from the movie, she could see that someone had left a bucket with a mop on the stage. Half the floor looked dusty, the other half clean, as if interrupted, Mr. Gorny had left the job undone.

She gazed around at the dark seats. The apparent emptiness was no consolation. The shadows were too deep, the opportunity to hide—and then leap out—too good. With each step she took down the aisle, her heart beat a little faster, her muscles tensed more, until she was clenching her fists so hard, her nails dug into the palms of her hands.

Turning, she glanced up at the little projector window and wondered if Mr. Gorny was up there. And where was Billy Brine?

At the end of the aisle, Alice climbed the steps to the stage. They creaked. Each sound sent chills down her spine. Chief Jimbo joined her, looking this way and that, obviously as nervous as she was.

Todd stayed below.

"I'll go check out the projection room," he said, and turned.

Then froze.

173

A figure emerged from the shadows, limping toward him. Billy Brine. He was wearing filthy clothes, and in one hand, held a long-haired wig.

In the other hand, he held a hunting knife.

"Don't move," he snarled.

Alice caught a rustle of curtain, and then, as she turned, she saw a shadow leap out of the wings and rush at Chief Jimbo. Mr. Gorny, his face twisted with anger, pulled out an identical hunting knife.

"No one touches this theater," he said.

Chief Jimbo reached for his gun. He patted his holster. Then groaned. "I left it in the car."

Billy snickered. Alice turned to him.

"Nice costume, Billy. Esther saw you take the shoes in her store. But then she was meant to. The shoes would be useful to stage Beau's death. And the theft itself could also point toward the so-called wild man of the woods." She nodded toward Todd. "Something Esther said stayed with me. The thief limped. Todd doesn't have a limp. In fact, he moves faster than a deer on those long legs. But someone else recently hurt their leg—when he staged his fall a little too realistically."

"Shut up," Billy hissed.

"But Billy didn't come to town until *after* Dorothy died," Chief Jimbo said.

"Because he was invited to come."

"Invited?"

"The killer, seeing an opportunity to connect Dorothy's death to an old murder case, used the shoes as a distraction. And then realized that wasn't enough. The Oz Killer story had to be so convincing that everyone wanted to believe it. Who better to throw the whole town off the scent than a true crime podcaster? Someone who could convince everyone that Arthur Crumpit was alive—and that the Oz Killer had struck again?"

"Billy knows the killer? How?"

Todd said, "Billy's his grandson."

Chief Jimbo's jaw dropped. "Mr. Gorny? Billy Brine? I never would've…"

"Shut them up, Billy," Mr. Gorny ordered, and Billy moved closer to Todd.

Alice said, "You can silence us. But you can't silence all of Blithedale."

The house lights flooded the auditorium. Billy looked around, a hunted expression on his face. Mr. Gorny's eyes strained in his face as the auditorium doors opened and people began streaming in. Becca and Ona first. Then came Andrea, Esther, Lorraine, Sandy, Mayor MacDonald, the Oriels, Althea and her bluegrass musicians, Thor, Susan, and dozens of others, until finally Beau stood in the entrance to the auditorium.

"Mr. Gorny," he said, his voice booming. "You're fired!"

"No," Mr. Gorny roared, and he leaped forward, raising the knife to strike Chief Jimbo. Alice, having no other weapon at her disposal, grabbed the nearest object—the bucket of water—and flung it wildly at the attacker.

Chief Jimbo jumped aside. The water struck Mr. Gorny in the face, and he screamed as if it had been acid. He dropped the knife and it clattered across the stage. He pawed at the sudsy water coursing from his eyes, which must burn. He cried out with a mix of rage and frustration and fell to his knees, and in the dark he looked like the wicked witch melting into a puddle of water.

"Ouch!" Billy cried out. "You're hurting me."

Todd had used the distraction to wrestle the knife from Billy, and was now twisting his arm, locking it behind his back. The knife lay on the floor.

Chief Jimbo stepped over to Mr. Gorny. He handcuffed him with a satisfying snap-snap. And for once, Blithedale's chief of police sounded confident as he said, "Mr. Gorny, you have the right to remain silent…"

Alice let out a long sigh of relief. It was over.

CHAPTER 37

"*L*adies and gentlemen," Beau said from the stage. "Let the show begin!"

As he walked offstage, the curtains swept back, and the spotlights glowed around the band. For this concert, the Pointed Firs—Althea and her band—had added a bass and a fiddle to the band. They struck up a foot-stomping bluegrass tune.

Alice grinned at Ona, who sat next to her.

"This is perfect."

Ona smiled and chewed, her mouth still full of pie. Outside in the lobby, Andrea Connor was serving apple pie and Becca plied people with coffee. People filled the auditorium. The whole town had turned out for the grand reopening of the Blithedale Theater—taking place on a Saturday afternoon, so everyone could enjoy the entertainment.

Three months had passed since Dorothy's killer, Mr. Gorny, had been arrested. Beau had recovered from the attack, and at once set about putting his sister's plans into motion. With financial support from the Blithedale Future

Fund, he'd quickly renovated and reopened the theater as a live music and performance venue.

Despite Mr. Gorny's murderous efforts, the Blithedale Theater was transformed.

Why Mr. Gorny had been so determined to preserve the movie theater remained for a prison psychologist to work out. In a very opinionated opinion piece in the newly relaunched *Blithedale Record*, Todd Townsend had suggested it was a combination of psychosis and entitlement. In fact, Todd had written, Mr. Gorny had devoted his life to the theater and felt as entitled to it as anyone in the Bowers family. When Dorothy hinted that change would come, Mr. Gorny invested in bringing Beau back into the fold. He knew the finances. It would take Dorothy years and years to transform the theater. But when Dorothy appealed to the new Future Fund, Mr. Gorny realized he'd run out of time. So he killed her.

He expected Beau to solve his problems, complying with his "savior" and his conservative vision for the theater. But Beau had seen the wisdom of Dorothy's plans, and Mr. Gorny, finally breaking with the Bowers family, desperately forced Beau to sign a will that left the theater to his grandson, Billy. Beau would have to die, too. The family tradition would continue—only it would be Mr. Gorny's own family carrying it on.

Mr. Gorny's madman dream had ended in a prison sentence for murder and attempted murder. Billy was convicted for accessory after the fact and for attempted murder. It emerged during the trial that he hadn't known about his grandpa killing Dorothy until after he came to town. Once he got up to speed, though, he did what he could to help Mr. Gorny get away with it.

Todd had published a scathing account of Billy's dubious research practices for his podcast. Apparently, he had planted "fresh clues" in other unsolved crime cases, claiming to have discovered new evidence. All in an attempt to "trend" as a podcaster.

"The desire for media success," Todd had written, "is a disease that has reached epidemic proportions. People will do anything to get a scoop. It's become a national perversion."

Todd apparently didn't see the irony that he—who had hidden in the woods as he worked on his own big scoop—accused others of going to great lengths to get an exclusive or trending story.

Alice leaned forward in her seat and, two rows down, spotted the gangly Todd with a notepad in his lap, scribbling notes on the performance. His hair was shorter, his clothes cleaner, and these days, no one would ever dub him a "wild man." He had succeeded in returning to town and opening his newspaper again, even if many people frowned when they saw him walk down the street, and Sandy Spiegel had threatened to break his arms and legs if he didn't return the bottle of bourbon he stole from her. Still, Sandy and everyone else read every word he wrote.

A simple "I'm sorry" might've cleared the air, but Todd was convinced he knew what the people of Blithedale needed: "a solid newspaper, not a bunch of sappy, sentimental words." Well, Alice and Todd would have to agree to disagree on that point.

She just hoped he would give the Pointed Firs a positive review. Althea and her bandmates were talented and deserved wider recognition. At least now that the town had its own music venue, these musicians had a home from which to develop their careers—and entertain the people of Blithedale.

Across the aisle, Lorraine and Sandy, sitting next to each other, were slapping their knees, both clearly enjoying the music. That was nice. Maybe Sandy would never enjoy *Grease*, but at least they could both share a love of Blithedale's own bluegrass music.

In front of them sat a man in a gray, rumpled suit. His feet, as he stomped along to the music, revealed Winnie-the-Pooh socks. In between the first two songs, Lenny turned and glanced back at Alice, giving her a brief salute.

She recognized many others in the audience—Mayor MacDonald in his white suit, sitting next to Mr. and Mrs. Oriel, Thor from the Woodlander Bar, even the purple-haired girls who had followed Billy Brine to Blithedale sat together, leaning against each other and bopping their heads to the music.

Here was a community worth investing in. And listening to. In fact, together, Alice, Becca, and Ona had developed a new process for the Blithedale Future Fund's applications. A more formal process that would include consulting the public to ensure anyone in town could share their opinion on which business they should support next.

It was a far cry from Alice's initial instinct to go it alone—or simply rely on the words of Old Mayor MacDonald for guidance.

Which is why it'll work, she reflected. *For all of us.*

After the first two fast-paced songs, the band launched into a heart-aching cover of "Over the Rainbow," and the auditorium grew still. With no one needing to speak a word, everyone understood who the song paid tribute to—the woman whose vision had led to the rebirth of the Blithedale Theater.

Alice felt her eyes growing wet. Then Ona wrapped her arm around her. As she watched the show through blurry vision, Alice sensed someone else sit down in the seat on her other side.

"Becca."

Becca put her arm around her, too.

As the band played, Becca and Ona leaned into Alice, the three friends holding on to each other, and Alice felt a warmth run through her, reaching down to the deepest recesses of her heart. She smiled at her friends.

"The dreams that you dare to dream," she whispered, "really do come true."

* * *

Thank you so much for visiting Blithedale. Join Alice and her friends for another cozy mystery in book 3:

A Halloween to Die For

Oh, and want a FREE short story? Sign up for my newsletter updates on new books and I'll send the free story to you by email:

https://mpblackbooks.com/newsletter/

Finally, if you enjoyed this book, please take a moment to leave a review online. It makes it easier for other readers to find the book. Thanks so much!

Turn the page to read chapter 1 of *A Halloween to Die For* (Book 3)...

A HALLOWEEN TO DIE FOR
EXCERPT

"*B*eware..." the ghostly voice said. "Beware..."

The ghost's torn robe fluttered in the chilly wind, the rags whipping around his knees. Old Mayor Townsend's bronze face was a sickly green. His eyes sparkled red as they gazed over Alice's head at Blithedale's Main Street.

"Too creepy?" Ona asked, popping out from behind the statue where she'd been hiding and pretending to be the old mayor's ghost.

"Is that one of the inn's bathrobes?"

"Yup. Torn to shreds."

"And the rhinestone eyes and the green face—well done."

"But temporary. If it rains, the green paint will run. I'll have to remember to reapply. So, what do you think?"

"Hmm...he still looks too—" Alice cocked her head. "—serious."

Ona stood next to Alice, regarding the statue. Then stepped up to the old mayor, dug into her pocket, and brought out a lipstick. She applied some to his face and stepped away.

"There. That's better."

"Much better." Alice smiled. "Now he looks friendly."

The statue of Old Mayor Townsend, decked out in a ghostly costume, now had a big red smile on his face. It made him look goofy and harmless, which was how Alice liked her Halloween.

Inside the Pemberley Inn, the phone rang and Ona rushed inside. Alice put another carved pumpkin with a light on the inn's porch. Ona's voice murmured through the front doors.

The wind gusted through Blithedale, and leaves of many colors tumbled down Main Street. Alice hugged herself. Next week, it would be Halloween, and each day it seemed to get a little colder.

She stepped inside the old Victorian mansion, shutting the door behind her. On a chilly day like this, entering the lobby of the Pemberley Inn, with its thick oriental rugs and cozy decor, felt like slipping into a favorite wool sweater.

Still on the phone, Ona said, "That's confirmed then—we look forward to seeing you on Friday." She hung up and beamed. "Eight guests. Eight! That means every single room at the inn is booked for Halloween weekend."

As she smiled, the red rhinestones on her eye-patch glittered. Alice couldn't help but smile, too. Ona's happiness was infectious. Yet a small, familiar voice in her mind scolded her for taking advantage of her friend. After all the time she'd spent in Blithedale, Alice still lived in the Colonel Brandon Suite upstairs, free of charge. But, as Ona had pointed out, Alice couldn't afford to pay and Ona couldn't afford to have her best friend move out of her house, so the arrangement was a win-win.

More of a win for you, the voice told her.

Alice ignored the old, critical voice. It might stay with her for many years to come, but she'd learned to listen to more sensible voices. Like Ona's.

Ona said, "Word is spreading about Blithedale. It's a long drive from the city, but people will gladly come for the fall leaves."

"And the pumpkins."

"Yes, and don't forget the haunted house."

Alice had seen the advertisements, of course. In fact, Ona had pegged one to the side of the reception desk:

Dr. Fantasma's Thrilling Adventures Presents:
The Blithedale Haunted House Experience.

The illustration showed an old ramshackle Victorian mansion tangled in cobwebs, with a skeleton sitting in a rocker on the front porch. Alice leaned closer. She'd looked at the poster several times before, yet there was a detail she'd never noticed before. Someone was peeking around a curtain at an attic window. The shrunken face of a ghoul, its eyes burning with malice.

The door to the inn banged open, and Alice's heart clenched. She spun around.

A man came through the entrance, pulling a small suitcase. He shut the door behind him with another bang.

He wore a dark suit, white shirt, no tie, and over that, a blue wool trench coat. His salt-and-pepper hair was perfectly coiffed, and when he smiled, he revealed teeth that would've made an orthodontist proud. He wasn't shy about showing them, either.

Alice, who'd pressed a hand to her chest, said, "You startled me."

"I should be the one to be startled." He looked from Ona to Alice, and then back to Ona again. "Blithedale is known for its natural beauty, but I see it's an understatement."

Alice glanced over at Ona. She pressed her lips tight. She was suppressing an emotion. Judging by the twinkle in her one visible eye, it was hilarity. The man's sweet talking didn't impress Alice, either, but she was more inclined to a grimace than a smile.

Ona consulted her computer.

"Welcome back, Mr. Conway."

"Stewart."

"I've got your room ready."

"I booked a suite."

"Are you expecting someone will join you?"

"You never know." That big smile flashed again as he stared at Ona. "You never know."

Ona ignored him. Alice leaned against the bottom banister of the staircase, watching the interaction. She'd met men like Stewart Conway before: wealthy, confident, and convinced of their own magnificence. She detested the type, but some women—incomprehensibly—absolutely loved guys like that.

Ona was detailing the many things to do in Blithedale on his visit.

"There's also a haunted house event," she concluded, gesturing toward the poster on the front of the reception.

"I know," he said. "It's my property."

"You're not Dr. Fantasma, are you?" Alice asked.

Stewart Conway looked over his shoulder at her and chuckled. "God, no. I own the properties Dr. Fantasma and his crew use for their so-called thrilling adventures. In fact, I own two dozen haunted houses across five states."

He looked around, studying the Pemberley's decor. A series of portraits graced the staircase wall, each one depicting a character from Jane Austen's novels. In the reception, there was a large framed oil painting of the fictional Pemberley—Darcy's estate in *Pride & Prejudice*—which bore little resemblance to Ona's Victorian mansion.

"I've always thought this inn was nice. I bet you do a good business."

"I do fine," Ona said modestly.

"How'd you like to expand? I've got a property that might interest you." He leaned against the reception counter, dropping his voice to a low, suggestive murmur. "I'd offer an excellent price—" He paused. Smiled. "—for a friend."

Ona grabbed the key to the room. "You've got lucky friends, Mr. Conway."

"Call me Stewart, please."

"Right this way, Mr. Conway."

Alice marveled at Ona's ability to be firm while still sounding friendly. She pushed back on Stewart Conway's come-on without giving him any cause for offense. Obviously, she'd dealt with the Conways of the world before— maybe even this Conway. Now she gestured for her guest to go ahead of her to one of the rooms on the first floor.

"Please, ladies first," he said.

Ona ignored it with a friendly smile. Finally, he gave a shrug and headed down the hallway, rolling the suitcase behind him.

There had been a moment there when Alice had wondered, worried, whether Stewart Conway was one of those men who got angry at rejection.

As Ona passed her, Alice whispered, "Want me to come?"

"He's harmless," Ona muttered, "unless you invite him into your room."

That sounded ominously as if Stewart Conway were a vampire. Alice watched Ona escort Conway down the corridor toward his suite. Well, if anyone could handle a bloodsucker, it was Ona.

After they'd vanished from sight, Alice continued to add Halloween decorations to the reception. She'd closed her bookstore, Wonderland Books, only an hour before, and darkness was falling outside. Once this job was done and things calmed down for Ona, they'd head over to the What the Dickens Diner for dinner.

Ona returned to the reception alone. When Alice asked her how it went with Mr. Conway, she rolled her eye. "The guy's got no shortage of self-confidence."

Ona expected no more guests that day. She had to prepare a room for an arrival in the morning, though. Alice helped her gather fresh linens, towels, and a bathrobe, and while Ona made the bed, Alice headed to the pantry off the kitchen to fetch a basket of complimentary goodies. This one had a Halloween twist: a tourist map of Blithedale, a small bag of candy, and a flyer advertising Dr. Fantasma's haunted house.

Alice was crossing the hallway to return to the room Ona was making up when she spotted Stewart Conway through the glass in the front door. Apparently, he was on his way out, but he'd stopped on the steps to talk to another man. Or that man had stopped him. They seemed to be having an argument.

Alice, pretending to need something from the reception, positioned herself by Ona's computer. She glanced over.

The men didn't seem to have noticed her. Stewart Conway had his back toward her, and the other man was too busy jabbing a finger in Conway's face. Conway's companion was a thickset man with the arms of a weight-lifter and a grim scar down one cheek. He jabbed the finger at Conway again, and even through the doors, she could hear his angry voice.

"You have no idea of the damage…"

Conway said something, maintaining a calm tone of voice. As a result, Alice couldn't make out the words.

"You bastard," the other man snarled. "You think because you own the property, you can do what you want."

Conway laughed and spoke again, once more too faintly for Alice to hear.

The other man clenched his fists and drew one arm back. For a moment, Alice was sure he was going to leap at Conway and punch him. But instead, he clenched his jaw and took a step away from him. He loosened his hands.

"We're talking about people's lives here," he said. Then he ran a finger across his throat in a threatening gesture. "Your own, too."

A chill went down Alice's spine as she watched the man walk away.

Want more? Join Alice and her friends in the next book: *A Halloween to Die For*

MORE BY M.P. BLACK

A Wonderland Books Cozy Mystery Series

A Bookshop to Die For

A Theater to Die For

A Halloween to Die For

A Christmas to Die For

An Italian-American Cozy Mystery Series

The Soggy Cannoli Murder

Sambuca, Secrets, and Murder

Tastes Like Murder

Meatballs, Mafia, and Murder

Short stories

The Italian Cream Cake Murder

ABOUT THE AUTHOR

M.P. Black writes fun cozies with an emphasis on food, books, and travel — and, of course, a good old murder mystery.

In addition to writing and publishing his own books, he helps others fulfill their author dreams too.

M.P. Black has lived in many places, including Austria, Costa Rica, and the United Kingdom. Today, he lives in Copenhagen, Denmark, with his family.

Join M.P. Black's free newsletter for updates on books and special deals:

https://mpblackbooks.com/newsletter/

Printed in Great Britain
by Amazon